PUFFIN

BEHIND THE SCENES

MEG TILLY is the author of three previous YA novels, *A Taste of Heaven*, *Porcupine*, and *First Time*. *Porcupine*—which was shortlisted for a BC Book Prize, the Canadian Library Association Best Children's Book, and *Foreword* magazine's Book of the Year Award—was named an Ontario Library Top Ten Best Bet in 2008. *First Time* was a 2010 CCBC Best Book, a Golden Eagle Award nominee, and a 2009 YALSA Quick Pick. Her adult novels are *Singing Songs*—a Barnes & Noble Discover Great New Writers selection—and *Gemma*.

Tilly is also known for her work as a film actress. Some of her better-known films include *The Big Chill* and *Agnes of God*, for which she won a Golden Globe Award and was nominated for an Oscar.

At present she is both writing and dipping her toe back into the acting world. She played Martha in the Blue Bridge production of *Who's Afraid of Virginia Woolf?* and Madeline 2 in Tarragon Theatre's production of *The Real World?* She has shot two seasons of Global TV's Canadian hit show *Bomb Girls*, which was awarded a Gracie for Best TV Drama. She was nominated twice for the Monte Carlo Golden Nymph for Best Actress TV Drama, and won two Best Actress TV Drama Leo Awards and the Best Actress TV Drama Canadian Screen Award.

Tilly has three grown children and lives in Toronto with her husband.

also by meg tilly

A Taste of Heaven

Porcupine

meg tilly

behind the scenes

PUFFIN
an imprint of Penguin Canada Books Inc., a Penguin Random House Company

Published by the Penguin Group
Penguin Canada Books Inc., 90 Eglinton Avenue East, Suite 700, Toronto, Ontario, Canada M4P 2Y3

Penguin Group (USA) LLC, 375 Hudson Street, New York, New York 10014, U.S.A.
Penguin Books Ltd, 80 Strand, London WC2R 0RL, England
Penguin Ireland, 25 St Stephen's Green, Dublin 2, Ireland (a division of Penguin Books Ltd)
Penguin Group (Australia), 707 Collins Street, Melbourne, Victoria 3008, Australia
(a division of Pearson Australia Group Pty Ltd)
Penguin Books India Pvt Ltd, 11 Community Centre, Panchsheel Park, New Delhi – 110 017, India
Penguin Group (NZ), 67 Apollo Drive, Rosedale, Auckland 0632, New Zealand
(a division of Pearson New Zealand Ltd)
Penguin Books (South Africa) (Pty) Ltd, 24 Sturdee Avenue, Rosebank,
Johannesburg 2196, South Africa

Penguin Books Ltd, Registered Offices: 80 Strand, London WC2R 0RL, England

First published 2014

1 2 3 4 5 6 7 8 9 10 (WEB)

Copyright © Meg Tilly, 2014

All rights reserved. Without limiting the rights under copyright reserved above, no part of this publication may be reproduced, stored in or introduced into a retrieval system, or transmitted in any form or by any means (electronic, mechanical, photocopying, recording or otherwise), without the prior written permission of both the copyright owner and the above publisher of this book.

Publisher's note: This book is a work of fiction. Names, characters, places, and incidents either are the product of the author's imagination or are used fictitiously, and any resemblance to actual persons living or dead, events, or locales is entirely coincidental.

Manufactured in Canada.

Library and Archives Canada Cataloguing in Publication data available upon request to the publisher.

ISBN 978-0-14-318251-1

eBook ISBN 978-0-14-319202-2

Visit the Penguin Canada website at **www.penguin.ca**

Special and corporate bulk purchase rates available; please see
www.penguin.ca/corporatesales or call 1-800-810-3104, ext. 2477.

To my husband, Don, with love

1
the phone call

"We need to talk." Alyssa's voice was low, muffled. Madison had to strain to hear through the earpiece.

"Sure, hold on a minute," Madison said as she headed for the kitchen door. Her little sister, Gina, had just rolled a Yahtzee with twos and was shrieking and hopping around the kitchen like someone had dunked her in a bathtub full of ice cubes. Madison slipped through to the back porch.

"Wait!" Gina bellowed, stopping in mid-celebratory hop, her head snapping around to fix on Madison. "Where are you going?"

"Alyssa's on the phone," Madison replied. "I'll be right back. Mom, could you roll for me?" Madison's mom nodded, Gina scowled and opened her mouth, but Madison closed the door behind her, the ruckus in the kitchen muted now, not as sharp and piercing. She held on to the doorknob, just in case Gina decided to come storming out. "Okay, Alyssa, I'm listening. What's up?" The doorknob wiggled, but Madison was prepared. She quickly leaned her body weight against the door and it stayed shut.

"No, not on the phone. Can you meet me?"

"Why are you whispering?" Madison asked, her stomach dropping, because now that she was outside, she could hear the strain in Alyssa's voice. "Is something wrong?" And a million worries suddenly flew through Madison's head. What if Alyssa's mom's weirdo stalker had found out where they lived and was holding them hostage? Stalkers were one of the many challenges that Alyssa and her mom had to deal with. "Do you need me to call 9-1-1?" Madison asked, her mouth suddenly chalk-dry.

"No," Alyssa said. "Nothing's wrong ..."

"Oh," Madison breathed, relief rushing through her. Madison had always thought it would be pretty cool to be famous. But ever since October, she had discovered that being famous had a downside as well. That was when Madison found out that Alyssa's mom was actually *the* one and only Jessica Ashton, a world-famous

Hollywood actress, who had arrived in their sleepy town of Rosedale to film the new TV show *Call Me Night*. "Thank goodness. You had me sc—"

"Actually," Alyssa cut in, "everything's wrong, but nothing that requires 9-1-1. Can you be at Willows Beach in … I don't know … say, an hour?"

"Let me ask my mom." Madison yanked open the door. Gina tumbled through and landed at her feet.

"You made me fall!" Gina roared indignantly.

Madison reached down and helped her up, even though it was Gina's fault, because, seriously, nobody asked her to lean against the door. "Sorry," Madison said, trying to sound contrite. Better to apologize than have Gina throw a hissy fit and get Madison in trouble. "Mom, can I ride my bike to Willows Beach?"

"We're gonna go to Willows Beach? Yay!" Gina said excitedly. "I *love* Willows Beach!"

"Not you," Madison said, frowning down at her sister. "Me."

"Madison, honey," her mom said, looking ready to refuse, "your dad was—"

"Please, Mom," Madison said, covering the mouthpiece of the phone. "It's important. Alyssa sounds upset, and needs to talk."

Madison's mom sighed. "All right," she said. "But I want you back by dinner."

Madison told Alyssa, then hung up and sprinted to her bathroom, grabbed a towel, and stuffed it in her backpack as she jogged down the hall to the front door. "You're the best, Mom!" she hollered super loud. Her voice overpowered Gina's small, plaintive, poor-me whine about how *much* she *loved* Willows Beach and *please, please, please* as she trailed after Madison in a woebegone manner.

But Madison was too smart for her. "Love you, Mom! Thank you *so* much! Bye!" Madison bellowed as she darted out of the house, shutting the door firmly behind her.

Madison coasted out of the driveway and turned left. It was the fastest route to Willows Beach. Usually on the weekends, Mrs. Bachrach, the neighbour up the block, kept her little Pomeranian, Rufus, on a leash or inside. But just in case, Madison kept her eyes peeled. She had been bitten by Mrs. Bachrach's dog when she was six and out biking with her dad. She had been feeling pretty proud because her dad had removed her training wheels, and she had almost managed to ride around the whole block without once falling over. Her dad had been a little ahead, doing fancy curving, sweeping turns with his bike, riding from one side of the road to the other and back again so he wouldn't get too far ahead.

Madison and her dad had ridden by Mrs. Bachrach's house many times before with no problem. But this particular morning, Mrs. Bachrach, still in her bathrobe and curlers, was leaning over her porch rail. She was chatting about the possibility of rain with Mr. and Mrs. Eckle in the next yard over, when little fluffball Rufus came tearing out of the door—yapping and snapping—and barrelled down the walkway toward Madison. At first Madison was worried because she wasn't very good at steering, and she didn't want to accidentally run over one of Rufus's little paws.

"Go away, Rufus!" she'd said. "Shoo!" And that's when he leapt—a blur of fur—and buried his jaws securely into the meat of her right calf. How he managed that feat was a mystery since he was only eight inches tall and she was on her bike, but he wouldn't let go, even when Madison and her bike crashed to the ground. Madison could hear her dad holler and knew he was coming, but Mr. Eckle got there first. He grabbed Rufus by the scruff of his neck. Rufus was jerking and snapping and trying to twist around and bite Mr. Eckle. Mrs. Bachrach was bashing Mr. Eckle over the head with her rolled-up newspaper and screaming, "Don't you hurt my baby! My defenceless little Rufus! Let him go or I'll kill you. I swear to god!"

Madison was standing there frozen, her whole body shaking and blood spilling down her leg, pooling in her tennis shoe, making it slippery and wet. Her dad scooped her in his arms, hugging and kissing her as he ran full tilt back to their house, jumped in the car, and drove like a maniac to the doctor's office.

Madison had to get ten stitches and a tetanus shot.

No, Madison was not partial to Mrs. Bachrach's defenceless little Rufus. When it came to that dog, she had learned the hard way not to leave anything to chance. And sure enough, as she approached, she saw old Mrs. Bachrach sitting on the stuffed armchair on the front porch, and Rufus running amok in the garden, lifting his leg on the lilac bushes.

Madison quickly yanked the handlebars into a U-turn, and none too soon. Rufus must have sensed Madison's presence: His head whipped up, his lips stretched into a sneer that displayed all of his tiny dagger-sharp teeth, and he charged.

Madison didn't waste one second. She stood up and pedalled hard. Soon the sound of his high-pitched bark faded in the distance, and it was just birdsong, wind, and the whir of her bike that filled her ears.

A short while later, Madison coasted up to the bike rack in front of the snack-shack and locked her bike. She didn't bother rounding the corner of the building to take a peek at the clock on the wall over the ice-cream freezer. She probably wouldn't be able to see it anyway over the heads of tall lanky teenagers and parents with their kids, all gathered around to purchase tasty treats.

Madison headed straight out to the beach. She was really early, but she hadn't wanted to hang around the house once she got the go-ahead.

The beach was a bit crowded, but that was to be expected on a sunny Sunday afternoon, especially with summer just around the corner. Luckily, a family was packing up. Madison waited patiently and nabbed their spot when they left. She pulled her towel out of her backpack and gave it a shake. A breeze off the water lifted the ends, making it ripple like a flag as Madison lowered it onto the sun-warmed pebbles. Then she slipped off her sneakers and lay down on her towel. The sun felt good, like a gentle embrace. The sea breeze turned the sticky sweat on her face and neck into a cool caress and caused her bare arms and legs to tingle.

Madison closed her eyes and breathed deeply. The slight tang, the smell of salt and seaweed, flooded her senses. She exhaled, breathed in again, even deeper this time. More smells entered the mix—sunscreen, cooking oil, greasy fries, ketchup. Mmm ... Too bad she didn't have any money.

There was a seagull's call up high to the right of her. The sound of pebbles shifting as someone padded by. The footsteps stopped.

"Maddie?"

Madison opened her eyes, her hand coming up to shade the sun. "Hey, Alyssa. You're early," Madison said, sitting up.

"So are you." Alyssa slumped down beside her on the pebbles.

Alyssa was wearing her jean shorts and a T-shirt too. *Funny,* Madison mused, *how we've started to show up wearing the same thing without even trying. Must be a best friend thing.* "Didn't you bring a towel?"

"Didn't think to." Alyssa was scowling out at the ocean.

"Well, here. You can sit on half of mine."

"Nah. I don't care." Alyssa flopped down on her back, her long blond hair splaying out across the pebbles like a mermaid's.

"Okay." Madison lay back as well. "Phew, it's hot," she said, acting like it was a normal day, like somehow that would stave off the bad news that was stewing in Alyssa.

Alyssa didn't respond.

"Can't believe it. Only two more weeks and we are done, done, done. Out of elementary school and on into sixth grade. Junior high!" And just saying the words, *junior high*, caused the breath to catch in Madison's throat. "I wonder what it's going to be like."

"Same but different," Alyssa said.

"Well, we won't worry 'bout it," Madison said, trying to tamp down a thrum of nervousness that was fluttering through her. "We've got the whole summer to get used to the idea. A whole summer to hang out, have fun, and—"

"I won't be here," Alyssa said, cutting her off.

"What?" Madison pushed up onto her elbow. Alyssa's arm was flung across her face, covering her eyes. "You're kidding, right?" A knot was forming in her stomach. "You're joking?"

Alyssa exhaled. Madison could see a muscle in her jaw jump. Alyssa opened her mouth, and her lips moved slightly, but no words came out. When they finally did, they were so soft that Madison almost didn't hear them. "I wish I was …"

2
bad news and dinner

"It's not fair!" Madison said, slamming the front door behind her. "It's just not fair!"

"Mom," Gina bellowed, bouncing out of the kitchen, "Madison's home!"

"Is everything okay?" her mom asked, poking her head out of the kitchen.

"No." Madison dropped her backpack on the floor and threw herself face down on the sofa. "Everything isn't okay. It sucks."

"Madison Stokes"—her mom's voice was sharp—"you watch your language."

"Sucks?" Gina piped up, looking curiously from her mom to Madison. "Is *sucks* a bad word? What's it mean?"

"Never you mind," her mom said. "Go help Daddy in the kitchen."

"But I want to stay. I wanna know *what's* not fair? Why is Maddie upset?"

Madison yanked her face away from the cushion and glared at her sister. "Go … away!" she said through gritted teeth.

"Hey, don't grouch at me," Gina said, backing up, her hands up like there was a water pistol stuck in her face. "I didn't do anything."

"Gina, the kitchen, now," their mom said.

Gina sighed and started marching toward the kitchen. "Meany-cabbeany," she muttered, screwing up her face, sticking out her tongue at Madison, and doing a butt wiggle. Of course she waited until she was behind their mom's back so she didn't get in trouble. Brat.

Her little sister disappeared around the corner as Madison's mom settled on the sofa beside her. "What's going on?" her mom asked.

Madison could hear the clank of dishes, cupboards opening and shutting, Gina's high voice and her dad's low rumbling one in the kitchen. There was something about those familiar noises that caused the ferocious anger that was storming through her to dissipate, leaving behind a sad sort of weariness. "Alyssa's leaving," she said.

"Oh dear." Her mom smoothed Madison's hair out of her face. "I'm so sorry, honey."

Madison opened her mouth, but there was a sudden ache in her throat that made words impossible.

"What happened, Maddie?"

"She ... her mom ..." Madison squeezed her eyes shut, trying to get rid of the stinging-hot feeling that threatened to engulf them. "The TV show got picked up for another season."

"Well, that's good, isn't it? That's what we were all hoping—"

"No!" Madison said, prickles of anger resurfacing. "You *don't* understand. We wanted the show to be picked up so Alyssa could *stay* here, but that's *not* what happened." Madison scrubbed errant tears from her cheeks. "The *stupid* network is moving the production to Los Angeles."

"But how can they do that?" Madison's mom looked confused. "The TV show takes place right here in Rosedale. It's part of the story."

"I don't know how they can do it, but they are. And you want to know the worst part of it?" Madison didn't wait for her mom to respond. "Alyssa and her mom are leaving in two weeks! The day after summer vacation starts. It's not *fair*! We had so many plans and now ..." Madison couldn't go on any further, she was crying too hard.

~ 13 ~

◇

Dinner was a subdued affair. Even Gina wasn't her usual blabbermouth self. It was just the sound of knives and forks scraping plates, of chewing and swallowing.

Well, other people swallowing. Madison was finding it difficult to get food past the lump in her throat. She knew her eyes must be swollen and her face blotchy and red because Gina kept sneaking worried peeks at her.

"Try to eat, honey," her mom said, reaching over and patting her hand.

Madison nodded, picked the drumstick off her plate, and took a bite. They were having her dad's famous oven-fried chicken with mashed potatoes, gravy, and corn on the cob. It was one of her all-time favourite meals, but not today.

She chewed, the chicken turning into lukewarm mush in her mouth. She tried to swallow. Wasn't working. She grabbed her water and took a big glug to help wash it down. She stared at her plate. *In two weeks Alyssa is going to be moving back to Los Angeles.* A fat tear splashed onto her plate, and then another. Madison tucked her head, hoping no one would notice. She pushed a splodge of mashed potato onto her fork.

She heard a chair push back, and felt her dad

come over. He wrapped his arms around her, his head resting on the top of hers. "I know it's rough, chipmunk," he said. "Your best friend moving away. It happened to me."

"It did?" Gina asked.

"Yup. Fourth grade. Kenny Freeman. My best bud since kindergarten."

"Did you cry too?" It was kind of a rude thing for Gina to ask, but Madison was glad that she did, because Madison wanted to know too.

"I don't remember." Madison felt her dad kiss the top of her head. His arms were warm and strong and comforting. "I do, however, remember feeling gutted, like life would never be the same."

"And was it?" Gina chirped. This confession of their dad's was seemingly cheering her up. "Was it bad? Was it never the same?"

"For awhile," their dad said, his voice thoughtful. "The summer was super tough. I had never not had a best friend before, and didn't know what to do with myself. I tried to do the same things I had done with Kenny. Your grandpa helped me with the tree house Kenny and I had been working on for two years. We actually finished it. And I love my dad, but it just wasn't the same—"

"Robert?"—their mom cut in—"Do you really think this is helpful?"

"Right." He cleared his throat. "What I'm saying is, it's going to be tough. No doubt. You're going to be sad and lonely, and rightfully so—"

"Robert."

Madison glanced up. Her dad had better be careful. Her mom had that warning look on her face that meant if he didn't shut up soon, he was going to be in big trouble.

"But, things will get better," her dad said. He didn't seem too perturbed, although he sped things up a bit. "Why, the very next September, your mother was in my class, and the rest ..."—he took a dramatic pause, a smile lighting up his face—"is history!" he said, swinging his arm in a wide, downward-sweeping, romantic, knight-in-shining-armour bow.

Unfortunately, his hand thwapped the handle of the large serving spoon that was stuck in the mashed-potatoes bowl, and a glop of gooey potatoes went flying through the air and landed, *splat*, in Madison's mom's startled face.

Everyone froze for a second. With potatoes slowly sliding down her face, Madison's mom said, in a dignified manner, "Robert, if that's the way you impress the girls ..."

And the next thing Madison knew, she was laughing. Then Gina too. Their mom looked so funny.

Her dad unfroze. "Oh …" he squeaked, leaping into motion, grabbing a napkin, zooming around the table—all gangly, awkward arms and legs—trying to get the offending goop off his wife's face. But she was having none of it.

"No," she said, holding up her hand, palm facing Madison's dad, as if she was the queen giving a royal command. "I think you have done enough," she said, pretending to be mad, but the corners of her mouth kept quirking up. "Although …"—her tongue flicked out and captured a dollop of sliding mashed potatoes—"I must say, you did an excellent job with these potatoes. The flavouring is …"—she kissed the tips of her fingers—"truly delicious."

Gina and Madison were laughing pretty hard now. Their dad was too, even though he was embarrassed.

Their mom picked up her napkin and began to daintily remove the mashed potatoes from around her eyes. "I must say, Robert, you do have a—"

The doorbell rang. Madison's mom's face switched in a split second from joking to horrified. "Oh my goodness! Who could that be?"

The doorbell rang again.

"Better get the door, Mom," Madison choked out between gasps of laughter.

"Not on your life!" her mom said, suddenly ferocious. "Robert, get the door," she roared as she dashed to the sink.

Madison leaned over to her little sister. "Gina, wouldn't it be funny if that was nosy Mrs. Krumboltz from next door!"

"Yeah!" Gina said, bouncing happily on her chair, her face lighting up like a Christmas tree.

"And when she saw Mom," Madison continued, "she thought, *Oooo, that must be the latest fancy beauty treatment*!"

"And she started wearing mashed potatoes all the time!" Gina squealed, the kitchen filling with her delighted laughter.

"Hello," a refined lady's voice said from the kitchen doorway. "I hope we aren't interrupting anything?"

"Huh?" Madison's mom swung around from the sink, water dripping from her face. Most of the potatoes had been washed off, but there were a couple of gooey clumps she had missed. The expression on her face when she saw who was in the doorway was priceless. As her mom lunged for a tea towel to vigorously scrub her face, a curious Madison turned to the door.

"Look who dropped by," her dad said with a big smile, his hands gesturing toward the surprise guests like he was a magician presenting a fluffy, white bunny he had just pulled out of a hat.

"Hey," Alyssa said with a cocky grin, ambling over to the table. "Yum. Your dad's oven-fried chicken. My favourite!"

"Alyssa …" her mom, Jessica Ashton, said, her face flushing. Although why she was looking embarrassed was a mystery to Madison. Jessica looked utterly perfect and beautiful, and *she* didn't have mashed potatoes and water slopping down *her* face. "That's not polite. One doesn't invite oneself to—"

"No worries," Madison's dad jumped in. "Lots of food for everyone!"

"Well," Madison whispered to Gina, quirking an eyebrow, "maybe not lots of mashed potatoes …"—which set Gina off into gales of giggles again.

Alyssa gave Madison a what's-that-about look.

"I'll … tell … you … later," Madison mouthed, her eyes sparkling.

Madison's dad was rearranging the table and adding two chairs.

"Oh, no, really—" Jessica Ashton said. "We didn't know it was your dinnertime. We don't want to barge in."

"It's no problem," Madison's dad said.

"Mom, please," Alyssa said, tugging her toward a chair. "He makes the best chicken, ever!"

"We'd love you to stay," Madison said. "The more the merrier. Isn't that right, Mom?"

"Oh yes," Madison's mom said, bringing two more place settings to the table. "It's not very hot, but we certainly have plenty."

Madison couldn't tell if her mom's face was red because she'd scrubbed it so hard, or if she was feeling shy because she had been caught looking … um … dishevelled.

"All right," Jessica said with a laugh. "We'll stay. Thank you so much. It is very kind of you. And I have to confess," she continued as they all took their seats, "it does smell divine. My mouth started watering the second you opened the front door and that delicious aroma wafted out."

"I've just got one warning," Gina piped up with her gap-toothed grin. "Watch out for my dad and flying mashed potatoes!"

3
maybe ... maybe not

"Your sister's cute, but, boy, I'm glad she's finally gone to bed," Alyssa whispered to Madison.

"Tell me about it." Madison rolled her eyes. She had been tempted to strangle the brat. Gina had spent the entire evening showing off and interrupting the grownups every two seconds with some antic or another.

Madison and Alyssa were sitting on the big black beanbag chair that was tucked in the corner by the TV, watching their parents talk on the other side of the room. It was hard to be quiet and not put in their two cents when the conversation the grownups were having would determine whether the girls had a glorious summer vacation or a terrible one.

"Will they let you come?"

"I don't know," Madison whispered back. But

she had a sinking feeling the answer was going to be *no*. Her parents were super protective. She doubted they would agree to let her jaunt off to California to stay with Alyssa and her famous TV-star mother for the summer. "Maybe."

Alyssa sighed and flopped backwards, causing the beanbag to adjust and tip Madison sideways. "I'll die if you can't come," Alyssa groaned. "Seriously . . . I'll *die*."

Alyssa's mom glanced over. "Well, someone's tired. I guess we'd better go. School tomorrow and . . ." Alyssa's mom said, taking a final sip of her tea and then setting her cup down and rising gracefully to her feet, "a five a.m. pickup for me."

Madison's parents rose from the sofa where they had been sitting, her dad's arm slung in a companionable way around her mom's shoulders. And maybe they didn't rise with the smooth fluid movement that Jessica Ashton did, and maybe they weren't as polished looking, but Madison was really proud of the way they had conducted themselves. They hadn't acted all tongue-tied or weird around Alyssa's mom. They just spoke to her like she was a normal parent.

"Five a.m.," Madison's mom said with a grimace. "I don't envy you."

Jessica laughed as they trooped toward the door. "Yes," she said. "Such a glamorous life."

Madison's dad opened the door. A moth that had been circling the porch light fluttered into the room. If Alyssa's mom hadn't been there, Madison's mom would have waved her arms and whatever else was handy and chased that moth back outside where it belonged. But she didn't. She just stood there with her arm tucked into the crook of Madison's dad's arm and with a gracious smile on her face.

Past the glow of the porch light and the warm yellow light spilling through the living room windows and out onto the lawn, Madison could see the glossy black town car with tinted windows parked by the curb. Maximilian, Miss Ashton's chauffeur, was leaning against it.

He glanced over, straightened, gave a slight tug to his already impeccable suit jacket, and rounded the car. He opened the back door and stood at attention, the interior light from the car illuminating the lower half of his legs and his shiny polished shoes.

"Thank you for a wonderful evening," Jessica said, shaking Madison's dad's hand. "Dinner was absolutely scrumptious. Clearly, Alyssa was not embellishing when she waxed lyrical about your culinary skills."

"Pfft," Madison's dad said, waving her compliment away like it was nothing, but Madison could tell by the way his chest puffed out a bit that he felt proud.

"And please, Kathy," Jessica continued, as she took Madison's mom's hand, "seriously, no pressure. It was a spur-of-the-moment idea, and I totally understand if it doesn't fit in with your family's summer plans."

Then Alyssa and her mom stepped off the porch and down the walkway, and disappeared into the waiting car.

Madison's mom put her arm around Madison's shoulders and nestled her in close. They stayed like that. Madison, her dad, and her mom on the porch watching the town car make a right-hand turn, the red tail lights vanishing into the night.

"Well . . ." Her mom took a deep breath and then exhaled noisily. "I don't know," she said. Her brow furrowed. "I just don't know."

"We don't have to decide tonight," Madison's dad said. "Come on, let's go inside."

And so they did. Madison kissed them good night and went to bed, even though inside she was jumping with excitement and possibilities and wanting to say, *please, please, please!* Her parents stayed in the living room, and she could hear the low rumble of their voices late into the night, until finally she fell asleep.

4
in limbo

The next morning, Madison was running late. She had fallen back to sleep after her mom had woken her. Probably because she had stayed awake so late the night before, wondering and wishing. She had to pedal full tilt on her bike all the way to school and arrived in class slightly sweaty and breathing hard just as her teacher was shutting the door. Alyssa glanced over at her, but before Madison could say anything to her, Ms. Elliot told Madison to take her seat, and the morning announcements began.

When the recess bell rang, both Madison and Alyssa were up from their seats and out of the classroom. They had discovered a few months ago that the trick to walking super fast without running was not to bend their knees. They looked ridiculous, but they didn't care, and this way, they never again got busted for running in school.

Once they exited through the door to the playground, they broke into a jog. "What did they decide?" Alyssa asked as they loped past the tetherball poles and the faded hopscotch.

"They haven't yet," Madison replied. The two girls crossed the field, climbed the slope, and sat down, the chain-link fence giving slightly as they leaned against it.

"You're kidding me? How hard can it be? Yes or no." Alyssa stared out across the playground, which was filling up with kids running, shouting, and bouncing balls. "I want you to come. You'd get to meet Nadine. You'd like her. She's a real sweetheart."

Madison nodded and smiled even though a wave of jealousy was washing through her. *What a bad friend I am*, Madison thought, shaking her head. She hadn't even met this Nadine person, and already Madison didn't like her because Nadine was going to be able to hang out with Alyssa and Madison wasn't. *I should be glad Alyssa has a friend waiting in L.A. for her.* Madison wasn't going to have anyone to hang out with. She sighed. It was going to be a long and lonely summer if her parents said no.

"What did they say after my mom and I left?"

"They said it was time for bed."

"They didn't discuss it?"

"Yes, but I was in my bedroom."

"Do you think they'll let you?" Alyssa asked, sitting up and propping her elbows on her knees. "They're going to say yes, right?"

Madison unwrapped her fruit leather, ripped off a piece, and handed it to Alyssa. "Well, you know my parents, they're kind of … um … cautious," Madison said. But truthfully, *cautious* wasn't really the right word for it. Madison's mom was freaking out.

Madison peeled off a piece for herself and took a bite. Her dad had made a bunch of homemade fruit leather in the fall when the store was having a special on apples. It didn't look like the store-bought stuff, but tasted better. He had added cinnamon, nutmeg, and fresh lemon to give it that perfect blend of tart and sweet.

"You *have* to convince them, Madison! It would be so much fun. We live in Bel Air, which is kind of blah, *but* in the summer, we always visit my mom's best friend, who has a beach house in The Colony—"

"The Colony?"

"It's in Malibu and *right* on the beach—"

"You're right on the beach now—"

Alyssa snorted. "I know, but the beaches in California are *way* different." She held out her hand for another piece of fruit leather.

"How different can it be?" Madison asked, pulling off another piece and giving it to her.

"Sandy beaches—"

"Oregon has sandy beaches too," Madison said.

Alyssa gave her a look. "Where?" she asked, arching an eyebrow.

"We do. Seriously. You just have to drive a bit."

"Well, at my mom's friend's house in The Colony, you just step off the sundeck and your feet sink into sand. And if you walk a little way up the beach, there's a great spot for surfing. And the water ..." Alyssa closed her eyes, her head tipped back. She exhaled with a peaceful smile. "It's sooo much warmer." She looked pleadingly at Madison. "You *have* to come. We'd have the best time ever and—" Alyssa sat up abruptly and grabbed Madison's arm. "Oh! And I forgot to mention, my mom said she'd be happy to pay for your ticket, so if money is an issue—"

"It's not," Madison said, even though it was. She could feel her cheeks heating up.

"Well," Alyssa said, looking at Madison closely, "tell your parents anyway, just in case."

Madison busied herself with the fruit leather, carefully pulling off another long strip.

"Okay?" Alyssa nudged her.

Madison nodded. Alyssa was watching her way too closely. "You aren't planning on telling them, are you?" Alyssa said.

"It might … I don't know … hurt their feelings or something. Make them feel like your mom thinks we're poor."

"No," Alyssa snorted. "Don't be silly. How could it hurt their feelings? You need a plane ticket. We have one. Simple. Promise you'll tell them."

Madison rolled up the strip of fruit leather and popped it into her mouth. "Mm …" she said.

But that wasn't enough reassurance for Alyssa. "*Promise*," Alyssa demanded.

Madison thought about the empty summer stretching out in front of her. She thought about Alyssa's friend Nadine waiting to step in and take over Madison's *best friend* status. "I promise," Madison said. And the minute the words were out of her mouth, she got a flutter of excitement that started to build. It *could* happen. She might be flying to L.A. with Alyssa and her mom in less than two weeks. Alyssa was right, why should Madison's parents mind who paid for Madison's ticket?

Alyssa smiled and leaned back aga[illegible] fence again. "Grrreat! It's going to be *fun*[illegible] can visit my mom's set. It's kind of bori[illegible] but since you've never been before, you might find it interesting for an hour or two. And Disneyland—we could go there. Have you ever been to Disneyland?"

"No," Madison said, shaking her head. She had seen ads for it, though. Magic dust and smiling faces and "The Happiest Place on Earth!" She had always wanted to go.

"Okay, well, we'll put that on the list." The recess bell rang. "Maximilian can drive us," Alyssa said as the two girls got to their feet.

They ran down the slope, back toward the school, with glimmering visions of Malibu, warm sandy beaches, Disneyland, movie sets, and a summer spent together dancing before them.

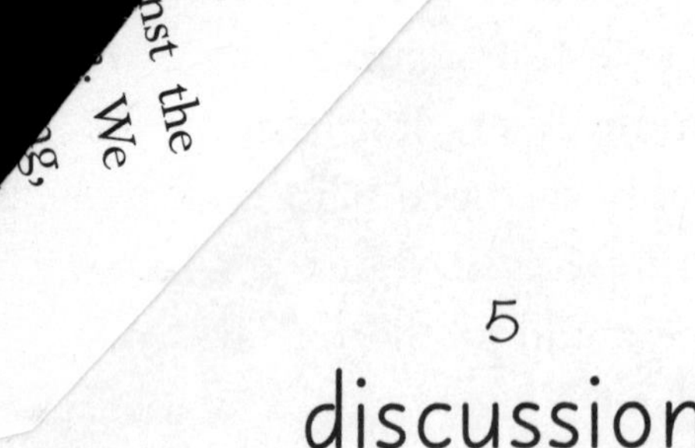

5
discussion

"I think she's too young," Madison's mom said, shaking her head. "It's a long way away." She tossed the can opener back in the drawer. "And didn't Jessica say, 'stay with us for the summer'? The kid's only eleven! It's a preposterous idea."

Madison finished wiping off the kitchen counters and moved to the fridge. Someone had left some raspberry fingerprints on it. It could have been Gina or it could have been her dad. She was working quietly and listening hard.

"Kathy," Madison's dad said from the kitchen table, where he had removed the outside layer of a computer and was fiddling with the guts, "it doesn't have to be for the whole summer. I agree with you on that. However, we shouldn't throw out the baby with the bathwater—"

"Pffft!" Madison's mom huffed, jamming a butter knife into the family-sized can of baked beans she'd just opened and prying up the lid. "I'll grant you that Jessica Ashton is lovely, and it was nice of her to offer to pay for Madison's plane ticket, but we could never accept."

"Why not?" Madison asked. "Her mom doesn't mind. It's no big deal. She's happy to—"

"Trust me," Madison's dad said, setting his screwdriver down firmly on the table. "It's a big deal to us, and it's not going to happen."

"Besides, the plane ticket is only one of my concerns," Madison's mom said as she dumped the beans into the cut-up hot dogs sizzling in a pan. "Even if we were able to come up with the money to buy a plane ticket, I'm not about to let Madison tromp off to L.A. to spend the summer in a house where the mother is never home. Jessica works such long hours. She wouldn't be around much . . ."

"Her housekeeper, Berta, is really nice too," Madison said, taking the can from her mom, peeling off the paper label, and putting it in the paper recycling.

"But she doesn't speak English, honey," Alyssa's mom said. "What if there was an emergency?"

"I'm sure," Madison's dad said, squinting over the top of his glasses at a tiny screw he was attempting to remove, "that the emergency personnel in Los Angeles would have a knowledge of Spanish."

"Alyssa speaks Spanish too," Madison said. "So if there was an emergency, she could interpret."

Madison's mother shook her head. "I just don't like it," she said, giving the wieners and beans a poke and turning the heat down. "Madison is too young to be supervised for the majority of the day by hired help."

"Mom, I'm eleven!"

Madison's mom puffed out more air from between her lips. "She turns eleven and thinks she's old," she said to the ceiling as she yanked open the fridge door.

"Besides, Alyssa said we were going to go to the set with her mom." Madison didn't mention the *hour or two* part of that conversation. "That would be really cool. I'd get to see first-hand how TV shows are made. A great educational opportunity!"

Madison's dad chuckled. "Nice one, Maddie," he said.

"Robert," Madison's mom said sternly. "We are supposed to be a united front."

"Not when I don't agree with you," he said,

rising and snagging her into a hug as she passed on the way to the sink to wash the head of lettuce in her hand.

"Robert," her mom said, tucking her face into his shoulder. She was keeping her voice low, but Madison could hear her anyway. "It's Hollywood. There are drugs and disreputable people and fast living and—"

"Mom, please," Madison said. She didn't mean to cut in. She was trying to be polite, show her mom how grownup she was, but the words burst out before she could stop them. "I really, *really* want to go. I've never been outside the state of Oregon, and I ..." She had to stop talking for a second, shut her eyes, and take a breath. "I just can't bear ..." The words came harder now. "... the thought of Alyssa moving back to L.A. and ... never seeing her again."

Nobody said anything. The kitchen was quiet. Madison made herself open her eyes and raise her gaze from the floor. Both her mom and dad were looking at her—really looking at her, looking deeper than the surface.

"I tell you what," her dad said. "This whole conversation might be a moot point. Let's price out the cost of a plane ticket and see what we're dealing with."

Her mother sighed. “The budget’s tight already, Robert. Forget about all of my other concerns. We don’t have the money to fly her to L.A. and back.”

“We’ll cross that bridge when we arrive at it,” he said, massaging some of the tension out of her mom’s shoulders. “Right now, I’ll clear my junk off the table so Gina can help her sister set it.”

After dinner, Madison shooed everyone out of the kitchen. “I’m going to do all the dinner cleanup by myself tonight,” she said. She figured the best way to convince her parents she was mature enough to be away was to be super responsible.

“All right, then,” her dad said. “Thanks, chipmunk.” Her mom and dad disappeared into their bedroom to look up information on plane tickets.

Madison cleared the table, did the dishes, and wiped the counters and the stove. She swept the floor and mopped it. Her parents were still in their room, so she got Gina in her pyjamas, and made her brush and floss her teeth and wash her face. She’d read her sister *Caps for Sale* and *The Story of Ferdinand* and was in the middle of *Where the Wild Things Are* when their parents emerged from the bedroom.

When she heard the sound of their bedroom door opening, Madison couldn't help the excited surge of hope that zipped through her body. But when they entered the girls' room, Madison could tell by the look on their faces that they were still undecided.

Suppressing a sigh, Madison finished reading to her little sister like it was an ordinary evening. Then she got her social studies homework from her backpack and went out to the kitchen while her parents stayed behind to kiss Gina good night and tuck her into bed. It was hard to focus, though. Madison's mind kept skipping back to Alyssa's friend Nadine, waiting for her in Los Angeles. What was she like? If Madison's parents agreed to let Madison go, would Nadine be friendly to her? And if she was, would Madison be able to put her unwanted twinges of jealousy aside and be friendly back?

Was Nadine's family rich and famous too? Madison sighed. She hoped not.

6
dollars and sense

The morning bell rang as Madison was snapping the lock shut on her bike. She ran to join the back of the fifth-grade lineup that snaked along the side of the school. Alyssa left her spot in the middle to meet her. "So?" Alyssa asked, head ducked, voice quiet. "Can you come?"

"I don't know yet," Madison said, keeping her voice low as well.

"What?" Alyssa shook her head in disbelief. "Why is it taking them so long? It's not that complicated—either you can go or you can't!"

"It's not that simple," Madison said, feeling a little embarrassed. "They've got to look at the budget and try to figure out—"

"But my mom said she would—"

"No, Alyssa. They aren't comfortable accepting."

"Why not?"

"It would feel like ..."—Madison shrugged—"I don't know. Charity, I guess."

"It's not charity," Alyssa said, shaking her head. "If anything, they would be doing the good deed to me, because I'm—"

"OH MY ... GOD!" Isabelle squealed at the top of her lungs. "You have GOT to be KIDDING me!" Of course everyone stopped talking and turned to see what the big deal was. Madison shook her head; she still found it hard to believe that less than a year ago she used to be pretty good friends with Olivia and Isabelle. But ever since Alyssa moved to Rosedale and Olivia and Isabelle decided to shun her, Madison stopped hanging out with them.

"No, I'm not joking," Olivia answered, with a smug smile on her face and her head tipped ever so slightly to catch the light. "It is one hundred percent true. My mother and I are travelling to Los Angeles to take part in a Kids ShowBiz Networking Seminar."

"Oh jeez," Alyssa groaned softly. "Give me a break."

"Can you imagine," Madison whispered back, "if she knew who your mother was?"

Alyssa rolled her eyes. "I don't even want to think about it. Honestly, it would be a nightmare."

Madison grinned. "Ooh … All those juicy networking opportunities she let slip through her fingers …" she said, wiggling her fingers at Alyssa like a wicked witch casting a spell.

Alyssa smothered a laugh. "You are a horrible person, Maddie."

"It is *very* expensive," Olivia continued. She was acting like she was talking to Isabelle, but she wasn't. She was making darn sure her voice was loud enough for the entire fifth-grade line to hear. "But *my* daddy says it's worth it."

"How much does it cost?" Isabelle asked.

"Twelve thousand dollars," Olivia said.

Joey Rodriguez whistled through his teeth. "You're getting ripped off, girl."

Olivia swivelled around to glare at him. "I am not, Joey Rodriguez. It is *very* exclusive! I had to send an audition tape and eight-by-ten headshots and everything."

"I don't care what hoops you had to jump through. If you're paying twelve grand for a vacation, you're getting ripped off," Joey stated flatly.

"It's *not* a vacation. It's a *working* holiday. You don't know squat. That twelve thousand dollars covers *everything* for nine whole days for me and my mom—hotel, meals, a tour of L.A., workshops," Olivia said, tipping her hand up so she could admire the sparkly polish of her manicure. "Not to mention meeting a real live casting director, child manager, *and* a genuine talent agent . . ."

Joey shrugged, unimpressed. "Then why mention it?" he said, looping a piece of old rope this way and that until he had fashioned what looked to Madison like a cowboy lasso. She wondered if it worked.

"Yeah, why mention it?" his best friend, Dylan, cackled, and it was like a spell had been broken: Everyone started to turn back to what they were doing before. The side door where they were lined up opened and there was their teacher.

"I think Joey's right," Alyssa whispered to Madison, as Ms. Elliot led the class down the hall toward their classroom. "Sounds like a rip-off to me."

It wasn't until later that the whole twelve-thousand-dollar conversation came back to haunt Madison. She had put the finishing touches on her "Pilgrims' Trip on the *Mayflower*" short report, so she sat back in her chair and scanned the room. She was the first one done. Ms. Elliot had instructed them to use a variety of three-, five-, and eight-sentence paragraphs and to alternate between simple and compound sentences. Madison glanced at the clock on the wall. *Goodness, there are still twelve minutes before the period is over.* She looked across the aisle. Olivia was hunched over her desk. She scribbled something down and read it over, her mouth moving slightly as she twirled a strand of her hair around her finger. "Arrgh!" Olivia muttered under her breath, an angry scowl on her face.

It's a good thing those Hollywood talent agents can't see her now. Olivia doesn't look so pretty when she's hunched over scowling like that. It would be a waste of her daddy's twelve thousand bucks for sure. Twelve thousand dollars … Madison thought, shaking her head.

And maybe it was the action of shaking her head that cleared it, or maybe it was just repeating that enormous amount of money in her head, but all of a sudden she got scared. If it cost Olivia's family twelve thousand dollars to send her and her mom to Hollywood for nine days, then how much would it cost to send Madison for the whole summer? Sure, she wasn't going to take workshops or meet casting directors and agents, but two months was way longer than nine days. Even if the cost was only two thousand dollars, there was no way Madison's family could come up with that kind of money. No way.

When the noon bell rang, Alyssa and Madison took their lunches outside to the playground.

They sat sidesaddle, facing each other, on two of the bouncing grey metal horses. Nobody ever played on them anymore. The Oregon rain had rusted the bounce out of their springs years ago. They must have been brightly painted, but now most of the paint had faded: Only the faintest traces of colour remained in the detailing of the saddle and the stirrups, and in the grooves of the horses' manes, tails, and hooves. Alyssa continued to chatter excitedly about California. "Not only that, my mom's friend Bev—well, her beach house is only a short walk to the Malibu Country Mart." She gestured with the pickle that came with her Nate's mile-high pastrami sandwich. "And there is this great little food stand that has the best chili dogs you have ever tasted."

The glare from the sun reflecting off the sand hurt Madison's eyes. Joey and Dylan were taking turns running along the teeter-totter, arms out for balance, trying not to fall. *Thunk* ... The far end of the teeter-totter landed hard in the sand.

"Hey?" Alyssa said. "Are you okay?"

"Yeah," Madison said with a shrug. "I'm fine." But she wasn't. She felt terrible. She should say something, not just sit there listening to Alyssa building castles in the sky about how glorious the summer was going to be and how much fun they were going to have.

"You aren't eating."

"I'm not that hungry," Madison said, lifting the flap of her slightly squished jelly sandwich. It looked kind of gross.

"Here," Alyssa said, leaning over and snagging her lunch bag off the ground. "There is no way I can eat this whole thing." She pulled the other half of her sandwich from the bag, unwrapped the white butcher paper, and held it out to Madison. "Go on."

"Nah, it's okay," Madison said.

Alyssa put it on Madison's lap. "You're being silly," Alyssa said. "It's going to go to waste."

The tasty smells of spicy pastrami, rye bread, mustard, and cheddar drifted up to Madison's nose and made her salivate, even though she didn't think she was hungry. "Thanks, Alyssa," Madison said. She sunk her teeth into the sandwich, and the taste on her tongue made her stomach growl happily.

"Whoa!" Alyssa said, reaching over and rapping on Madison's belly. "What do you have hiding in there? A tiger?"

Madison's stomach gave another loud gurgle, which caused both girls to laugh. "I must have been hungry and not even known it," Madison said, feeling a little sheepish. She took another bite. Yum. It was good.

7
california dreaming

Two more days had passed, and still, Madison's parents hadn't come to a decision. They were at Grandma and Grandpa's house, the entire family around the kitchen table watching Madison's grandpa slosh warm brandy over the meringue topping of the Baked Alaska. "And now," he said, "the pièce de résistance!"

"Alfred," Madison's grandma admonished, "not so much … the children."

"Ach …" he said, waving her off, adding another splash for good measure. "The alcohol burns off. Besides, they like the fireworks—don't you, kids?"

"Yes sirreeee!" Gina shouted. "We like lots of flames. It's pretty!" Her scrawny arms were flying over her head and her fists were pumping in the air like Grandpa was the hero at a football game.

"Lights!" he told Grandma, even though he didn't have to. She was already standing by the light switch on the wall. She flicked it off. The kitchen was darker, but they could still see because the days were longer now.

"Are you ready?" Grandpa asked Madison, his eyes twinkling. He was hunched over like a sorcerer right before the big reveal, the match poised dramatically at the side of the matchbox.

Madison smiled and nodded her head.

He struck the match along the box and the tip burst into flame.

"Here we go, here we go!" Gina squealed, hugging herself with glee.

Grandpa waved the match next to the dessert. "Abracadabra!" he said, and suddenly the Baked Alaska was covered in shimmering, dancing blue-tinged flames.

"Ooooh … Ahhh … So beautiful!" everyone said.

Madison looked at her family gathered around the dessert, the flickering flames illuminating their faces. *I'm so lucky,* she thought. It was so sweet of her grandpa and grandma to make such a special dinner. Her mom and dad must have told them about Alyssa's invitation and how reluctant and sad it made them that they were going to have to tell her they couldn't afford it. *They're probably waiting to give me the bad news after dessert.* The flames got smaller and smaller until, finally, the last one flickered out, and the room was dark again. It was a second before anyone said anything or moved, all of them still caught up in the lingering beauty of the moment before—with the smell of burnt sugar and brandy, and the promise of dessert-to-come dancing in the air.

Then Madison's grandma got up, her slippers making a soft shuffling noise as she went over to the light switch and turned it back on. Everyone blinked as their eyes adjusted.

Her grandma got a large knife from the drawer. Madison's mom got a stack of saucers, and within a matter of seconds, they all had a generous wedge of delicious Baked Alaska sitting in front of them.

Everyone watched as Grandpa designed his first forkful, making sure he got a bit of the cake, a dollop of meringue, and a dab of all three ice creams—strawberry, chocolate, and vanilla—and put it in his mouth. "Mmm ... Ruth, my love," he said, raising his fork in the air like a sceptre and rolling his eyes in ecstasy, "you did it again!" He always did that. It was tradition.

Then everyone dove in with gusto, and it wasn't long before every last scrap was gone.

"Well …" Madison's dad said, pushing back from the table, his chair tipping onto its back legs.

"Robert," Madison's grandma said, rapping her knuckles on the table.

"Oops!" he said, quickly settling his chair back on all fours. The expression on his face made Madison laugh. He looked like Gina when she got caught sneaking cookies. He cleared his throat. "Okay, now," he said, cracking his knuckles. "About this trip …"

Suddenly, Madison realized that everyone was looking at her—her mom, her dad, her grandma, her grandpa. Even Gina, after glancing around the table, was now staring at her.

Madison felt her cheeks heat up. "Um," she said quickly before he could finish what he was going to say. "It's okay. I totally understand. It's too expensive. I already figured it out."

"Honey—" Madison's mom said, a faint smile on her face.

"No, seriously," Madison said quickly, holding up her hand. "I had no idea how expensive it was, or I never would have asked. And I don't want you to feel bad. I've already decided I don't really want to go anyway. California? Who cares.

It would probably get boring after awhile, and I'd miss all of you, so really, it's a lucky thing we can't afford it!" Madison made herself smile big, like she was really happy about it all, but kept her gaze cast down so they couldn't see the truth in her eyes

No one spoke.

Madison looked up from her plate. The grownups were looking at her with bemused smiles on their faces.

"Hmm ..." her grandpa said, getting up and going to the corner of the kitchen to the desk where her grandparents did the bills. "That's a problem," he said, rummaging through the perpetual stack of mail and stuff. He pulled something out of the pile. "Because what are we going to do with this?" he asked with a grin.

Madison looked at the business-envelope-sized folder her grandpa was holding up. His hand was covering most of it, but she could see red and white and lettering in black, and the part of the word she could see had *-line* on it. Could that be for *Airline*? Her heart started beating super fast in her chest, her hand rose and pressed up against it, and the other hand flew to her mouth. "Do with what?" she asked, barely daring to hope.

"This round-trip plane ticket to Los Angeles,

California," he said, with a huge smile on his face. He sauntered over to the table and dropped the plane ticket in front of her. "We got the flight information from Miss Ashton herself. You, my dear girl, are going to be leaving for L.A. a week from today."

"Oh my … Oh my!" Madison gasped.

"Now, before you get too excited, you need to know something," Madison's dad said. "This is not for the whole summer. After a lot of discussion, we settled on just shy of two weeks. We figure that's long enough, considering it's your first time away from the family."

"That's great!" Madison felt like a jack-o'-lantern all lit up. "I didn't think I was going to get to go at all."

"Will you look at her face?" Madison's grandma said, turning to smile at her husband and patting one of his wrinkled hands with one of her own. "If that isn't happy, I don't know what is."

"How did you afford it?" Madison asked.

"We all pitched in," her dad said. "Your grandma and grandpa, your mom and me."

"Mom? Are you okay with this?" Madison asked. "Really and truly?"

Her mom nodded, smiling, wiping a tear

from her eye. "Our baby's growing up, Robert," she said to Madison's dad.

He kissed the top of her head, and then rounded the table. "But," he chuckled, wrapping Madison in a huge hug, "if you *really* don't want to go—"

"I do. I do. I do!" Madison exclaimed, tears and laughter coming at the same time. "Thank you! Thank you so much!"

The rest of the evening passed in an excited blur of hugs and kisses and more laughter and more tears. Everyone crowded around the phone as Madison called Alyssa and told her the news. Alyssa screamed so loud she almost blew out Madison's eardrum. Madison had to hold the phone about a foot away from her head, and even then, she and everyone else in her grandparents' kitchen could hear Alyssa's excited shrieks and laughter as clear as a bell!

8
landing in l.a.

The first thing Madison noticed when she followed Alyssa and Alyssa's mom out of the Los Angeles airport terminal was the traffic. Cars zoomed past, horns honked, and engines roared as cars, taxis, buses, and limousines jockeyed for position, zigzagging in and out—the smell of exhaust fumes was thick in the air. There were four lanes of traffic under the concrete overhang, then a strip of raised sidewalk where pedestrians waited for the second set of traffic lights to change so they could safely cross the next five or six lanes of traffic beyond that.

Next, she noticed the heat. It was different from Oregon's humid summer heat. This was dry, hot heat, and it didn't originate just from the sun overhead. It seemed to be emanating from all the concrete buildings, sidewalks, and roads as well. It reminded Madison of the heat that escaped from the oven when she opened the door.

It was hard to believe she was actually there, *in* Los Angeles. The last week had zipped past in a frenzied blur. She must have packed and unpacked the old brown suitcase her grandpa had lent her a million times.

On her last night home, she came into her bedroom, and everything she'd packed so carefully was dumped out on the floor. "For Pete's sake!" Madison exclaimed. "What a pest!" Madison marched to her suitcase, scooped up an armload of clothes, and flipped open the lid, but there was no room for clothes because her little sister, Gina, was curled up asleep inside.

"I want to go with you," Gina said, a woebegone expression on her face as Madison carried her gently to her bed.

"I know you do," Madison said, tucking Gina in. "Maybe when you're bigger, you can go to L.A. too."

"I'll miss you," Gina said, wrapping her arms around Madison's neck.

"I'll miss you too," Madison said. And the odd thing was, she had meant it.

And now here she was, in L.A., with her little sister and her family so far away. Everyone in L.A. seemed to move so fast, and appeared to know exactly where they were going. A jumble of bodies, baggage carts, a cacophony of noise, and there, across the street was a row of real live palm trees—"Oh my goodness," Madison murmured. They were much taller than she had imagined and so odd looking with their long skinny trunks and blob of palm fronds at the top. She nudged Alyssa and pointed. "Very Dr. Seuss, don't you think?"

Alyssa laughed. "Come on, slowpoke," she said, tucking her arm through Madison's. "The light's changed." They hurried so they wouldn't be too far behind Alyssa's mom, who was moving fast. She was wearing a hat and large sunglasses that were so dark Madison couldn't see her eyes behind them. But the hat and the glasses hadn't done any good, because the paparazzi had found her anyway. Half a dozen of them were circling her in a feeding frenzy with a flurry of cameras clicking and flashes flashing. "Miss Ashton … Miss Ashton!" they yelled, which didn't help matters. The more they yelled and the more the cameras clicked, the more other people's heads swivelled in their direction.

"This way, Miss Ashton! Give us a smile!" But Alyssa's mom didn't stop. She just kept walking fast with her head down, as Maximilian and another equally large man in a dark-coloured suit cleared the way.

"How did they find out she was going to be here?" Madison asked.

Alyssa shrugged. "Don't know, but they usually do. Especially when the studio puts us on American Airlines. My mom thinks someone who works there earns extra money on the side by selling the information about which stars are flying and when." They had crossed the street and were entering a concrete parkade.

"That's terrible," Madison said. It was a little cooler now that they were out of the direct sun, but not much.

One of the paparazzi managed to shove past Maximilian and stuck his video camera right in Alyssa's mom's face. "Miss Ashton!" he shouted. "Would you like to make a statement regarding the rumours swirling around you and Ted Swick? Are you dating?"

"No," Alyssa's mom said, her voice firm and her face set.

Maximilian pushed his body between Alyssa's mom and the rude paparazzo and forced him back.

"That's not what Mr. Swick says," the paparazzo chortled, holding his camera up high over

Maximilian's shoulder. "Why don't you just come clean?"

"Yeah," another paparazzo yelled, her long, greasy grey hair flapping around as she jostled for position. "Have you met his wife and kid?" Without skipping a beat, she dodged around a couple that was exiting the elevator. "Were you aware that she is six months pregnant with their second child?"

They had arrived at a sleek, glossy, black stretch limo. Alyssa grabbed Madison's arm and pulled her around the back of the limo to the other side and yanked open the door. "Get in. Get in," she said, keeping her head tucked down and turned away from the cameras.

Madison hopped in the limo. There were forward- and backward-facing seats. "Where do I sit?" she asked.

"Anywhere! Just grab a seat," Alyssa said, giving Madison a little shove from behind. Madison plopped down on one of the backward-facing seats. It was fancy inside. There were magazines and a bar with a little fridge and a crystal decanter half-filled with an amber-coloured liquid.

The bodyguard in the dark-blue suit opened the door for Alyssa's mom to get in. "Do you really think it's fair," the greasy-haired woman paparazzo yelled, "for you to steal her husband? How is she expected to—"

Jessica Ashton whirled around. "I don't want her husband!" And to Madison inside the limo, it sounded like Alyssa's mom was close to tears. The rest of the paparazzi closed in like hyenas on a kill, the camera flashes accelerating to a blinding torrent. "I've *never* wanted her husband!" Jessica said, her voice fierce. "Get your frigging facts straight." And then she was in the car, with the door shut solid behind her. The cameras still flashed, but she didn't look at them. She didn't look left or right, just stared straight ahead in the direction of the headrest of the empty limo seat in front of her.

The limo backed up. The driver had to go slowly so they didn't run the paparazzi over.

"What about Maximilian and the other guy?" Madison whispered to Alyssa, who was in the seat next to her mom.

"They're picking up our luggage," Jessica Ashton said. Her voice was pleasant, but there was strain on her face. "We'll meet up with them at the house."

"Oh," Madison said. It was kind of a dumb response, but she didn't know what else to say.

The limo wove its way through the parkade, and Madison watched through the rear window as the paparazzi got smaller and smaller, until finally they were gone.

No one spoke. There was just the whir of the tires on the asphalt and the sound of the air conditioning filling the limo with cool air.

"You know . . ." Alyssa's mom said, her hands twisting in her lap as she turned to Alyssa. "What that paparazzo said is not true. Ted Swick is not my boyfriend. He never was—"

"I know, Mom," Alyssa said, cutting her off, storm clouds rising in her eyes.

"They just make stuff up—"

"I know, Mom! Jeez. I'm not a little kid," Alyssa said, turning to stare out the side window, her arms crossed tight across her chest. "I am aware of how things work."

Alyssa's mom opened her mouth like she wanted to say something more. But she didn't—only sighed, shut her eyes, and tipped her head back against the headrest.

It was a little uncomfortable for Madison sitting in the seat opposite them, because no matter which way she turned her head, someone was in her line of vision. She didn't want it to seem like she was gawking at their family squabble, so she loosened her seat belt and turned around so she was kneeling on her seat and peering through the darkened glass to the front of the limo. Which would have worked fine, except the limo driver pushed some button that made the glass slide down. "Do you need something, miss?" he asked. "Is everything okay?"

"No, I'm fine," Madison replied, breezily. "Just was curious what the view was like looking this way. You don't have to have the glass down. I can see perfectly well."

"Oh dear, honey," Madison heard Alyssa's mom say. "Do you get carsick?"

"Oh, no, no, I'm fine," Madison said. "I wanted to enjoy the limo ride from all angles—"

"There's no need to feel embarrassed, sweetie. Lots of people are uncomfortable riding backwards. Why don't we change places?"

"No, really, I'm—" But it was pointless for Madison to continue to protest, because Alyssa's mom had already unbuckled herself and moved to a backwards-facing seat, and was strapping in.

"Go on," Jessica said with a smile, making little scooting motions with her hand.

So Madison switched seats. "Thank you," she said, her cheeks hot. *Mom would be horrified*, Madison thought, *if she knew I accidentally kicked Jessica Ashton out of her seat.*

9
danger in paradise

"Ahh ..." Jessica Ashton said, rolling her shoulders and stretching her arms outwards as the limo slowly glided through the wrought-iron gates and up the long circular driveway. "It's good to be home." Her cell phone jangled out a tune. Alyssa's mom rolled her eyes. "It never stops," she said, unzipping her purse and rummaging through it for her phone.

The limo eased to a stop in front of a huge pale-grey mansion. The gutters lining the roof, the window and door trim, and the doors were painted a fresh white.

"Hello?" Jessica's mom said into her phone. "No, I'm back in L.A. now. We just arrived."

Madison cracked open the limo door. She could hear the deep guttural growl of a big dog barking, but it didn't sound super close. It must belong to a neighbour.

"You okay?" Alyssa asked.

"Yeah," Madison said, taking a deep calming breath. She opened the door wider and stepped out of the limo. The heat outside seemed even hotter than before. "Wow," Madison said, taking another deep inhalation. "It smells so pretty. Different from home." Fragrant white flowering gardenia bushes, white calla lilies, and lavender were growing alongside the house. There was a small tree next to the house that matched the large tree in a grassy area in the middle of the circular driveway in front of the house.

The barking sounded closer. *Focus on your surroundings,* Madison told herself sternly. *You are fine. You are totally safe. There are no crazy dogs here.*

Alyssa started to exit the limo. Madison took another calming breath. "Um …" she said, "lovely." Both trees had smooth undulating limbs with peeling bark, its colour a mixture of grey, beige, and rust. The leaves were a pale silvery green-grey. At the base of the big tree, a profusion of lavender grew. *Mom would like this,* Madison thought. And thinking of her mom and how much she liked flowers gave Madison a pang of homesickness. *This is silly,* she told herself. *I haven't even been gone a whole day yet!*

WOOF ... WOOF ... WOOF! Madison heard and then she saw it! A huge slathering Rottweiler with enormous teeth and a spiked leather collar came tearing around the side of the house.

"WATCH OUT!" Madison screamed. She whirled and shoved the exiting Alyssa back into the limo.

"What on earth?!" Jessica Ashton sputtered as Alyssa landed sprawled across her lap. But there was no time to explain. Madison dove into the limo as well and yanked the door shut in the nick of time. That dog had been so close she could smell its foul meaty breath.

The beast leapt up, its gigantic paws banging on the roof of the limo. ON THE ROOF OF THE LIMO! That's how big it was. It was barking and whining and slobbering its great drooling tongue all over the window, leaving slimy saliva smears all over it and giving Madison a clear view of its enormous incisors and the damage they could do.

"The dog ..."—Madison was having difficulty catching her breath—"There's a dog out there." Madison untangled herself from where she had landed on Alyssa and slid to the corner of the limo furthest from where the dog was going wild. She was a little embarrassed, but proud too, because she had saved the day. Sure, they got banged around, but what if that dog had hurt them? What if it had ripped their throats out and killed them? That would have been terrible.

10
nadine

Jessica and Alyssa pushed themselves to a sitting position. Nobody was saying anything. They were probably in shock. The Rottweiler was still going crazy outside, but Alyssa and her mom weren't looking at the dog. They were looking at each other. Madison felt a cold sweat flush through her body. Something was off.

"Did I hurt you? Are you okay?" Madison asked, suddenly anxious.

"That dog, there?" Alyssa asked, pointing out the window. "That's what you saved us from?"

"Uh … yes," Madison said, cautiously.

Alyssa started laughing, and after a second, her mom did too.

"Well, that's a really good thing," Jessica Ashton said, tugging her skirt back into place and slipping her foot back into her sling-back shoe. "Because knowing Nadine, she probably would have licked us to death."

"That's ... Nadine?" Madison swallowed hard. "Nadine's a dog?"

"Yes, you goofball," Alyssa said, opening the door of the limo.

The dog lunged in, weird sort of whining moans escaping from deep in its throat, its body a contortion of wiggles. It had a laughing Alyssa pinned against the seat of the limo and was drowning her face in exuberant licks. "Blech ... Nadine, stop!" Alyssa giggled. "Get her off me!"

"Wow," Madison said, her back stiff and a smile plastered on her face, like she hadn't just made a big fool out of herself and wasn't terrified out of her skull to be this close to an enormous, slobbering dog who had the capability to destroy her. Not to mention the fact that she had spent the last week and a half being jealous of a non-existent person. "You have a ... a dog," she said. "Cool."

Jessica tugged at the gigantic beast's collar to no avail.

"Sorry, Miss Ashton." A stocky old man, with a weathered, wrinkled face and bushy white hair, came shuffling around the corner. "Nadine," he said in a strict voice, shaking a gnarled finger at the dog. "Release!" Nadine immediately leapt out of the limo and plopped into a sitting position beside him. "That was no way to greet Miss Alyssa." He took a secure hold on Nadine's collar. "Come on out," he said, peering into the car. "I've got her now. Welcome home."

"Hello, Fred," Miss Ashton said, getting out of the limo. "Was Nadine okay while we were gone?"

"The dog was good as gold. Missed you a bit. Howled at night, so I let her sleep in the caretaker's cottage with me and the missus. And who is this?" he asked, turning to beam at Madison, who had just exited from the vehicle. Madison smiled back. He reminded her of her grandfather—a kindly sort. Not only that, but he *was* holding the dog and that was *definitely* a good thing!

"Madison is Alyssa's friend. She's come for a visit," Alyssa's mom said.

"Lovely to meet you," Fred said, wiping his hand on his muddy coveralls and reaching out to shake Madison's hand. "Fred Barkley at your service—handyman, gardener, jack-of-all-trades."

"Fred keeps this place running," Jessica said with a smile. "I don't know how we would manage without him."

"Nice to meet you," Madison said. Her heart

was still pounding pretty hard. Nadine was a dog. A *huge* dog with big teeth.

"Hi, Fred," Alyssa said, jumping out of the limo and wiping the dog-slobber off her face with her forearm. "Come on." Alyssa tugged on Madison's arm. "I'm boiling hot. Let's go for a swim."

"I . . . I don't have my swimsuit," Madison said. She was feeling kind of discombobulated. Her legs felt like jelly. "It's . . . uh . . . in my suitcase."

"No worries," Alyssa said, walking through the front door. "You can borrow one of mine."

"Okay, thanks," Madison said, following Alyssa inside. The coolness in the house was a welcome relief from the heat outside. Not to mention the solid front door closing firmly behind them, leaving Nadine-the-crazed-Rottweiler on the other side. Madison didn't get a chance to look around. Alyssa was moving at breakneck speed into the fancy foyer, up the stairs to the second floor, and down the hall.

"Here's my room," Alyssa said, flinging the door open and disappearing inside.

Madison followed, her brain and body still recovering from the dog drama. *Alyssa has a dog. Not just any dog . . . A humongous man-killer dog.* She took a deep breath. *Let it go,* Madison told herself. *The dog is outside. You are inside. You are safe.*

She made herself relax. The room was painted a pale barely-there hyacinth with rich cream window frames. Alyssa's bedside tables and desk were cream as well, with hyacinth knobs as an accent colour. There were two armchairs tucked in the corner with a side table and a lamp. The four-poster bed had sheer cream curtains that were pulled back in a swoop with a silvery tasselled cord. The bed looked soft and luxurious.

"This is like a fairy-tale room," Madison said.

"It's okay," Alyssa said with a shrug, walking over to a door and opening it.

Madison peeked inside and her breath caught. It was a huge walk-in closet with floor-to-ceiling built-in dressers and hanging racks filled with beautiful clothes. At the far end of the closet was almost an entire wall of shoes, boots, sandals, and flip-flops. "Wow," Madison said, taken aback. She never would have known Alyssa had this many clothes. "Did you buy all this?"

"No," Alyssa said, dropping to her knees. "My mom likes shopping." She pulled out a dresser drawer and started rummaging through it.

"Mm ..." Madison nodded. She put her hands in her pockets. Took them out again. That dog could have bitten off her fingers with one quick snap of her teeth. "I didn't know you had a dog," Madison said.

"Yeah," Alyssa said, removing a bunch of swimsuits and spreading them on the floor. "We've had her since I was five."

"Huh," Madison said, trying to sound casual. "I wouldn't have taken your mom for a dog person."

"She wasn't," Alyssa said with a snort. "Neither of us was, but we love Nadine now." She sat back on her heels and gestured at the swimsuits. "Which one do you want?"

"Is there a swimsuit you usually wear?" Madison asked.

"Nah," Alyssa said. "I'm easy. If you like one, take it."

Madison picked up a polka-dot aquamarine two-piece. The ties around the neck and at the back had adorable fringe tassels dangling at the ends. It was the prettiest swimsuit she'd ever seen. "Are you sure you don't mind?" she asked. "If it's your favourite you'd tell me, right?"

"Pfft ..." Alyssa puffed through her lips. "Madison, you're so funny. I've never worn that swimsuit. Look." She pointed to a sales tag that Madison hadn't noticed dangling from the swimsuit bottoms.

"Oh," Madison gasped and plopped the swimsuit back on the pile, her face heating up. "I'll find another. I didn't know." How rude

Alyssa must think she was, trying to wear her brand new swimsuit.

"Madison," Alyssa said, picking up the swimsuit and shoving it back into Madison's hands. "Don't be crazy. I've never worn it because I don't like it. Not that it's ugly or anything—it's just not my style. My mom was on a shopping jag, and I guess she felt the need to bring something home for me."

"But if I show up wearing it, won't it hurt her feelings?"

"I doubt she'd even remember." She gave Madison a gentle shove. "Go put it on. Your room is on the other side of the bathroom," Alyssa said, squatting down and snagging a swimsuit from the pile. "You can just walk through. Meet you in the hall in five."

Madison's room was almost exactly like Alyssa's, except it was painted a pale barely-there pink. It had the same chairs, same four-poster bed, same swoopy curtains and tassels, same fluffy cream carpet on the hardwood floor. There were similar lamps and silver-framed, old-fashioned flower prints. The pillow propped up on one of the armchairs was a different colour, but seeing the two rooms side by side—so similar—was weird. It made Alyssa's room feel not so special.

She heard a bark outside the window and felt hope surge. Maybe the dog wasn't allowed inside? That would be doable. She'd just have to make sure not to go outside unless the dog was tied up.

Madison got changed and headed to the hall. Alyssa was already waiting, leaning against the wall in a faded old swimsuit—which was classic Alyssa. She had a whole drawer full of dream swimsuits, and she found and wore the only shabby one. "Hey, slowpoke," Alyssa said with a grin, handing Madison a thick plush towel. "The swimsuit looks cute on you. You should keep it."

"You're crazy," Madison said, wrapping the towel around her and tucking in the corner. "My suitcase will be here soon, and I've got two perfectly good swimsuits." She didn't mention that the two swimsuits she packed were her only swimsuits—and before last week, she only had one swimsuit to her name. The second swimsuit was a special going-away gift from her mom and dad and Gina. "How long will it take to get to the pool?"

"Not long," Alyssa said, linking arms with Madison as they headed down the hall.

"Car? Bike?"

"Hmm ..." Alyssa stopped, and screwed up her face, thinking for a second. "I think we'll walk," she said, the corners of her mouth quirking.

"Okay."

They reached the foot of the staircase, but instead of going out the front door, Alyssa turned left. *There must be a path in the back that leads to the road,* Madison thought as she followed behind. *I wonder how long a walk it is.* She glanced into the living room on the right as they passed. It was very fancy, all taupe and pale sage. There were leather armchairs with velvet ottomans and sofas, and window seats in plush fabrics. She could see a fancy fireplace with a large gilt mirror over the mantel, candles set out in glass containers, and several vases of fresh cream-coloured roses displayed around the room. *No,* she thought, a feeling of peace washing over her. *That dog is definitely an outdoor dog. There's no way they'd let that tornado loose in here!*

They moved on, past a library with floor-to-ceiling books and a big desk and cozy nooks for reading, past the formal dining room, through the kitchen where Berta was at the sink washing vegetables, and on to the breakfast room. Madison was just about to follow Alyssa through the door to outside when Nadine loped around the corner of the house, her long pink tongue with black spots lolling out of her mouth. She gave a loud woof.

Madison quickly pulled the door shut.

Alyssa turned. She looked surprised. "Maddie?" she asked, peering through the multi-paned French doors to where Madison was standing stock-still in the breakfast room. "Are you okay?"

"Sure," Madison said, breezily gesturing in the air with her free hand, the other one still firmly gripping the doorknob. "I was just thinking maybe the whole swimming thing—"

Alyssa squinted at her suspiciously. "Are you scared of dogs?"

Madison opened her mouth to deny it, but no words came out.

"You are, aren't you?"

Madison nodded.

"She's really gentle," Alyssa said, slinging an arm affectionately around Nadine's neck. She didn't even have to bend, that's how big the dog was. "You don't have to be nervous. She doesn't bite friends."

"Oh … good …" Madison said, trying to smile. But seriously, the fact that the dog "didn't bite friends" was not very comforting. Because that meant there was a whole slew of other people that Nadine must bite on a regular basis.

Madison felt a trail of clammy perspiration trickle down her back. Her mouth felt dry and chalky.

"Come on out." Alyssa gestured encouragingly. She scratched the dog behind the ear. The dog grinned. Nadine had a lot of teeth. "You'll see how nice she is."

And Madison wanted to come out. She wanted to show Alyssa how brave and fearless she was, but when she tried to turn the doorknob and move her legs forward, her body refused.

"Aquí," the housekeeper, Berta, said, nudging Madison behind her. She stepped out to the patio, shutting the door behind her. *"Ella está asustada. Voy a poner el perro en el apartamento de Max mientras nadas."*

"Bueno," Alyssa replied, nodding her head. *"Buena idea. Gracias."* Alyssa was bouncing from foot to foot. *Oh dear, she must be getting impatient with me. You've got to get over this dog thing,* Madison told herself sternly. *It's really dumb.* But still she wasn't able to step outside.

Berta looped her hand under Nadine's collar. *"Bueno, permite ponerse en marcha,"* she said, giving a tug, and then Berta and the dog disappeared around the corner.

Madison opened the door a crack. "Is the dog coming back?"

"Nope. The coast is clear," Alyssa said. "Berta's putting Nadine in Max's apartment over the garage."

"Oh." Madison let out the breath she'd been holding. "Okay." Madison stepped gingerly outside to the patio. She could hear the trickle and splash of the fountain. The slate tile on the ground was hot under her bare feet. *Ah,* she thought, *that's why Alyssa was doing that little shuffle dance. She wasn't impatient with me—her feet were hot.* The two girls scampered quickly to the lush grass beyond, the heat and the fragrance of the garden air engulfing them. They rounded a corner and Madison stopped in her tracks. She couldn't believe what was before her. "You … you have a pool?" she finally croaked.

"Yup," Alyssa said, removing her towel and sticking her toe in the water.

"Why am I surprised?" Madison said, shaking her head. After all, Alyssa's mom had a driver, a housekeeper, a groundskeeper with his missus, and a huge mansion. Of course they had a beautiful, pristine, postcard-perfect swimming pool!

"Ah … good temperature," Alyssa said. "Not too cold, not too warm." She tossed her towel on one of the cushioned teak loungers and dove in.

She was a good diver. There wasn't even a splash.

"*This* is super cool!" Madison said with a grin. She tossed her towel onto the glass-and-chrome table with the large extended grey umbrella hovering above. "Bombs away!" she yelled, and then leapt out over the sparkling blue water, grabbed her knees, tucked her head, and landed in the water. It was a very satisfying cannonball. Someday she'd learn how to do a proper dive, but for now, it was fun just to make a huge splash.

11
too much sun

"Alyssa, honey," Alyssa's mom said, as she delicately placed a serving of slender grilled stalks of asparagus on her plate. Madison was impressed how she managed it so effortlessly. When Madison had attempted to get some of the asparagus on her plate, they'd skidded around and one flipped up in the air and landed on the fresh tablecloth. She's snatched it up quickly with her hand and plopped it on her plate, but grease marked the spot where it had lain. "It appears you girls forgot to apply sunscreen."

Madison glanced guiltily at Alyssa, who was sitting opposite her. Alyssa opened her mouth, but her mom held up her hand.

"Don't bother denying it. You are redder than a cooked lobster. This is not good. It's Madison's first night here, and you both are burned to a crisp. Have you put on aloe vera?"

"Mom …"

Alyssa's mom shook her head. "That means no." She pushed back her chair and stood up. "Come on, we'll do it now. You too, Madison."

Alyssa scrunched down in her chair. "Mom, we're eating."

"The food will be okay. You're going to be uncomfortable already, but the longer you wait to apply the aloe vera, the worse the burn will be. Come on," Alyssa's mom said in her no-nonsense voice. "Hop to it."

Madison stood up. Alyssa groaned, but she got out of her chair. They followed Alyssa's mom into the kitchen. "If I've told you once, I've told you a million times—you must wear sunscreen when you go outside."

"It's so slimy and gross," Alyssa said. "And I hate the feel and smell of it. It coats everything with this thick yucky goo, and my skin starts to feel claustrophobic."

"Claustrophobic?" Alyssa's mom said, quirking an eyebrow, her mouth trying not to laugh. "Well, you certainly are an original, my dear."

Alyssa scowled at her mom, who had turned back to the industrial-sized stainless-steel fridge and pulled open the door. "However," Alyssa's mom continued, "claustrophobic skin is preferable to skin cancer. Ah! Here it is." She removed a bottle of aloe vera from the fridge and swung the door shut. "And not to harangue you about it ... but, sweetie—seriously—too much sun is one of the things that will age a woman's skin very fast."

Alyssa heaved a heavy sigh.

"I know you don't care about it now, but when you get to my age, you'll care a whole lot more. Smoking, drinking alcohol to excess, and too much exposure to the sun's harsh rays are surefire ways to be a wrinkled old prune well before your time," Alyssa's mom said, plopping the bottle of aloe vera in Alyssa's hand. "Do you girls need help putting it on?"

"No, Mom," Alyssa replied, stomping out of the room. "We aren't babies."

"Don't forget to do your backs!" Alyssa's mom called after them as they headed down the hall. "You can help each other."

"Argh!" Alyssa said, slamming the bathroom door shut. "She drives me crazy sometimes. Who cares if I get wrinkles? I'm not going to be a stupid actress when I grow up. I'm going to be something useful."

"You do look a little burned," Madison said.

"Whatever," Alyssa said, unscrewing the

bottle and placing the lid on the counter. "You first."

Madison stripped down to her bathing suit. "Whoa," she said, glancing in the mirror. "I am burned. Weird. I wasn't this red when we came inside."

"Yeah, that's because with sunburn your skin keeps burning even after you come inside." Alyssa glanced at Madison's back and let out a long whistle. "Mom's right," she said, grudgingly. "It's good we're putting this on." She poured a generous glug of aloe vera into her cupped hand. "Ready?"

Madison nodded.

"Here we go." Alyssa stepped closer and smeared the handful of chilled slimy gel on Madison's back.

"Aaahh!" Madison shrieked.

"Hold still," Alyssa said, trying not to laugh.

"It's *cold*!"

"Come on now, stop dancing around!" Alyssa said, trying to be stern. "You're making me slop this stuff on the floor." But the strict act just wasn't cutting it, because Alyssa was out-and-out laughing.

"Okay, okay," Madison said, forcing herself to stand still. "I'm ready. Go ahead and do it." Alyssa smeared another generous handful of ice-cold aloe vera across Madison's back.

"Aahh . . . Aahh . . . Aahhh!" Madison squeaked, but she managed to hold still, even though it was a severe shock to her system. "It's really, really cold," she said.

"Stop whimpering," Alyssa said, snort-laughing. "You're such a baby."

"Yeah," Madison said through chattering teeth. "Just wait until it's your turn. Then we'll see who's a baby."

12
homesick

"Okay," Madison said. "I love you too. I miss you. Night-night." She carefully placed the receiver back in its stand. She stayed for a moment, sitting on the tall stool by the phone in the darkened kitchen. The dishwasher, hidden by a matching wood panel that blended seamlessly with the surrounding cupboards, purred and swished softly as it washed the evening's dishes.

Madison knew she should join Alyssa and her mom in the living room, but she needed a bit more time to pull herself back together. She hadn't expected the wave of loneliness that crashed over her when she heard her family, excited about her trip, asking questions about the plane ride and Los Angeles and what it was like. She told them about stepping out of the airport that afternoon and seeing the palm trees. She told them about the heat and the traffic and the enormous multi-lane freeways and the mansion Alyssa and her mom lived in with the beautiful gardens and the swimming pool.

"A swimming pool?" Gina had squealed. "Lucky!"

Madison's mom was interested to hear about all the flowering plants and made Madison promise to take lots of pictures.

But it was her dad she couldn't fool. It was her dad who said, "Whoa … wait a minute. Back up. Did you say a *dog*?"

"Yeah," Madison had said breezily. "They've got a guard dog—"

"What kind of dog?"

"A Rottweiler …"

"Oh jeez." His voice sounded like he'd just swallowed a bug. "You've got to be kidding me! I can't believe Jessica didn't think to mention that salient fact."

"It's not her fault. They didn't know I was scared of dogs. The subject never came up."

"Still," her dad said with a sigh. "Are you okay?"

"Oh yeah, Dad. I'm fine," she lied. "Don't worry." But even as she said it, her eyes had filled up because she wasn't fine, and the sudden missing of him made her throat close.

And now, sitting in the kitchen, she could almost see his kind face with his slightly wonky glasses and the laugh lines around his eyes.

The kitchen door swung open. "Maddie?" Alyssa said, poking her head through. "You done?"

"Uh-huh," Madison said, hopping off the stool. She arranged her face into a smile and followed Alyssa into the living room.

The change in light made her blink.

"How's everyone at home?" Alyssa's mom asked.

"Oh, fine," Madison replied. "They send their love and wanted to make sure that I thank you for letting me use the phone."

"Anytime, dear," Jessica Ashton said with a yawn. She put down her magazine and rose to her feet. "Well," she said, "I think I'll have an early night. Don't forget to turn the lights out when you girls are done." Which was another thing that was way different than at home. Alyssa got to decide when to go to bed, whereas Madison's parents had strict bedtimes for both her and Gina, except for a super-special occasion like tonight when they knew Madison was going to call.

As Jessica moved around the glass coffee table and bent over to give Alyssa a kiss good night, the phone rang. Jessica ambled over to the phone by the piano and picked it up. "Yes?" she said.

Madison glanced over and wished she hadn't. A myriad of emotions flitted across Alyssa's mom's face in quick succession, going from cozy-sleepy to what almost looked like a flash of fear. A second later it was gone. Her eyes had narrowed; her mouth was a hard unyielding line. "How did you get my home number?" Alyssa's mom demanded, her voice ice-cold. "It's unlisted."

Alyssa looked over at her mom, her head tilted to the side slightly and her thighs tense, like she was warring with herself whether or not she should get up and go to her mother and try to help.

"I have asked you, again and again," Alyssa's mom said, "to leave me alone."

"Who is it?" Madison mouthed.

"I don't know," Alyssa mouthed back, then added in a whisper, "Sometimes crazy fans get our number, maybe it's—"

"I am *not* interested. I have *never* been interested!"

"No," Alyssa whispered. "I don't think it's a—"

"Well"—Alyssa's mom gave a brittle laugh—"that's between you and your rampant imagination. And nothing to do with reality. *No,* that was a business dinner. One dinner, which my child and her friend attended. It was most definitely *not* a date. And for the record, I would never date you. Never mind that I find you repulsive, but add to that the fact that you have a wife, a child, and another baby on the way—it's really a no-brainer!"

Alyssa's eyes widened. "It's the creep!" she said, her voice low. "The one the paparazzi keep saying she's having an affair with."

"Well, she's obviously not," Madison whispered. "Just listen to her. Sounds like she hates him."

"She does," Alyssa said with a nod. She took a deep breath and cupped her hands around her mouth. "MOM!" she bellowed. "I NEED YOU. I'M STUCK!" she yelled, flinging herself on the floor and wedging her body under the coffee table. "HELP!"

"I have to go," Alyssa's mom said. "My daughter needs me. Do not call here again." She hung up the phone and spun around. "Alyssa? Are you all right?" She ran over to where Alyssa was sprawled. "What on earth happened, honey?" she said, starting to lift up the end of the coffee table. Alyssa scrambled out before she got the table more than two inches in the air.

"Don't worry, Mom," Alyssa said, dusting herself off. "I was just giving you a good excuse to get off the phone."

"You little scamp," Jessica said, affectionately ruffling Alyssa's hair. "What am I going to do with you?" She dropped a kiss on Alyssa's brow.

The phone rang.

They all froze.

"I'll get it." Jessica marched over to the phone and picked it up. "Hello?"

She listened for a beat and then slammed the receiver back down.

Brrrrring ... *Brrrring* ... It was the phone again.

"Don't pick it up," Jessica said, her face tense. "No one pick it up. Just ignore it."

"Mom," Alyssa said, reaching over and disconnecting the cord, "just unplug it."

"You're right," Jessica said with a rueful laugh, pulling Alyssa in for a hug. "Clever cookie."

Brrrrring ... *Brrrring* ... went the phone in the kitchen. Alyssa grimaced. "I forgot. We have more than one phone." They trooped into the kitchen and disconnected that phone.

Brrrrring ... *Brrrring* ... went the phone on the patio, the phone in the study, the phones upstairs.

"Wait!" Jessica said, stopping Alyssa in the

process of unlocking the patio door. "This is ridiculous. We can't unplug every phone in the house."

"Yes, we can," Alyssa said.

Brrrrring . . . Brrrring . . .

"But what about tomorrow? And the next night?" Jessica shook her head. "Are we supposed to live without a land line for the rest of our lives?"

"We have cell phones," Alyssa said.

Brrrrring . . . Brrrring . . .

"No!" Alyssa's mom said, slapping her hand down on the counter. "It's not okay for us to let this creep harass us in our own house." She stalked over to the intercom and pressed a code.

"Yes?" Maximilian's voice came over the intercom. Jessica explained the situation. "I'll be right over," Max said.

By the time Max arrived at the house, the ringing had stopped. "Don't worry," Jessica said. Her face was a little pale, and she was rubbing her temples like she had a headache coming on. "It's a temporary lull."

And sure enough, no sooner had Max sat down in the chair behind Jessica's desk in her office when the phone started ringing again. Maximilian picked up the phone, his face like thunder. Madison and Alyssa couldn't hear what he said, but they could see him through the thick glass panes in the office door. He looked scary, immovable. It became very clear to Madison that she would *not* want to ever piss him off.

The phone didn't ring anymore that night.

Max went back to his apartment over the garage. Jessica went to bed, and Alyssa showed Madison her art studio in the basement. There were paintings everywhere—glorious paintings hanging on the walls and stacked against the walls, and a half-finished one on an easel.

"You did all of these?" Madison asked. "How on earth did you find the time?"

Alyssa shrugged. "After school, spring break, summer vacations."

It's summer now. Madison felt her face flush. She was cutting into Alyssa's painting time. "If you want to paint anytime while I'm here," Madison said, "don't worry about me. I can always read a book or—"

"Madison, you nut," Alyssa said affectionately. "I didn't invite you here so I could lock myself into my room and be an 'artiste,' I'm going to hang out with you. Once you're gone, I'll have the rest of the summer to paint."

"Are you sure?" Madison asked.

Alyssa nodded. "I'm positive," she said.

"All right," Madison said. "But if inspiration strikes, promise me you'll go right ahead."

"Okay."

Next to Alyssa's studio, there was a media room that looked like a miniature theatre with big armchairs and a TV that practically covered a whole wall. "Do you want to watch a movie?" Alyssa asked.

"Which one?"

"I don't know," Alyssa said, opening a cupboard. Its shelves were completely filled with DVDs. "Any one you like, or we could play Yahtzee?"

"Let's do that," Madison said, because there were so many movies to choose from, she had no idea where to start. It was a little overwhelming.

So, they went upstairs and played Yahtzee and talked about what a creep Ted Swick was. Madison pretended to be having fun, but it had been a long day. As the evening wore on, she developed a pretty bad headache herself, and her body was throbbing from sunburn.

Finally, a little after ten, they grabbed the aloe vera from the fridge and trudged upstairs. *Bed,* Madison's body groaned. *Need bed. So tired.*

But sleep didn't come. She had lain in bed for hours, twisting and turning. Her pyjamas were clammy and sticky from all the aloe vera she had slathered on. It hurt when she moved and hurt when she lay still. To make matters worse, Nadine put up a howling ruckus when they had walked past the laundry room, until finally Alyssa's mom got out of bed and made Alyssa go down the hall and retrieve the dog.

"I'm sorry," Alyssa had said, holding on to Nadine's collar with both fists as the dog strained toward Madison. "She's always slept in my room and we've been away and she's missed me …"

"It's fine," Madison replied. "No worries." But she kept her fingers tucked into her palms and behind her back so Nadine wouldn't decide on one for a nice bedtime snack.

"I'll keep her in my room," Alyssa promised. "I'll keep the bathroom doors shut. Don't worry—I won't let her slip into the bathroom on the sly."

"Sounds good," Madison said.

But it wasn't. Because as she lay there in bed, she could hear Nadine pacing around Alyssa's room and snuffling her nose along the bottom of the bathroom door. She snuffled loud. Like she was hungry. Like she was thinking about busting the door down.

It was not restful.

Finally, the dog settled down. The whole house had gone to sleep. Everyone but Madison.

There was a silver clock on the bedside table. It had a very loud *tick … tock … tick … tock …* It was like water torture, the noise seeming to getting louder and louder until Madison opened up the drawer and stuck the clock inside.

Still she couldn't sleep.

The room was so big and unfamiliar. The house made a lot of noise, shifting and cracking as it settled. Did it make that much noise in the day and no one heard it? Or was it just noises that came out at night? *Boom … thump …*

Madison's dad said houses made noises at night because of the change in temperature outside. And he was probably right … but what if he wasn't? What if the noises here were different kinds of night noises? Ghost noises …

Or maybe one of Miss Ashton's stalkers had bypassed the security and was going to murder them all in their sleep?

"No more!" Madison said, throwing the covers off and sitting up. "I can't take it." She marched across the room toward the bedroom door. Miss Ashton said she could use the phone anytime? Well, she was going to call her dad!

WOOF! Nadine barked.

"Aaah!" Madison levitated a good five inches into the air. She heard the clang of Nadine's choke chain as the dog shook her head and rose from where she must have been lying. Madison froze. She could hear the click of Nadine's toenails as she stalked across the floor. Madison turned her head. Looking through the bathroom, illuminated by the glowing seashell night light, she could see the dark shadow of Nadine's nose as she started her snuffling search along the thin space between Alyssa's door and the floor.

Madison had two choices. She could either continue on her mission to the kitchen to call her dad and wake him up. *And*, in the process of doing that, wake up Alyssa and her mom and maybe even Berta, the housekeeper, depending on where her room was—because there was no way that stupid dog wouldn't bark big-time if she continued out to the hall. Or, she could turn around and very quietly tiptoe back to bed.

She tiptoed back to bed, but not before she firmly shut her bathroom door. *Dumb dog!*

13
gooey eggs

Alyssa's mother smiled at the girls as they entered the breakfast room. She was wearing a luxurious white robe over a long, cream-coloured silk nightgown. Her hair was tousled from sleep and her face was freshly washed, and she looked absolutely gorgeous. "Did you sleep well?" she asked, taking a sip of her coffee.

"Great, thank you," Madison replied, because what was she supposed to do? Tell the truth? That she'd had a horrible night of *no* sleep, thank you very much, and tonight probably wouldn't be any better!

"Nadine was so funny," Alyssa said, digging into her Eggs Benedict with relish. "She slept on the floor right by my bed instead of on her cushion. And she had her head tipped up so that her nose was resting on the bed." She laughed.

"She was sneak-being-bad, but I didn't let her. I told her no in a stern voice, and she skulked her head down again."

Madison smiled like she thought that was funny too and that Alyssa had told a cute story. But really, she was grouchy that the dumb dog was so stubborn about sleeping in Alyssa's room.

Alyssa shoved another mouthful of the gooey Eggs Benedict into her mouth. "Yum ..." she said. "This is one of my favourites." She beamed at Madison sitting opposite her. "Maddie, I'm so glad you were able to come. We are going to have the best time ever!"

"Yeah," Madison said. She stared down at her plate. Her mom and dad would never give her gooey eggs with oozing yolks. They knew she needed her eggs cooked super hard. The thought of her mom and dad and little sister and the familiarity of home made her stomach ache and her eyes feel hot. She poked gingerly at the egg with her fork. It jiggled. It looked sort of like fancy sauce on a big pile of snot. *How am I going to get through two weeks of this?*

Madison sighed and rotated her plate. *No, the eggs are just as gooey from this angle.*

Berta hadn't served Alyssa's mom gooey Eggs Benedict. She'd given her some fresh fruit and a blob of cottage cheese. Maybe Madison could get that instead? Not that she was a big cottage cheese fan, because cottage cheese looked kind of like something someone had thrown up, but at least she could eat the fruit.

No. That might seem rude. It was obvious that Eggs Benedict took a bit of effort to cook.

"What are you girls going to do today?" Alyssa's mom asked, spearing a ripe strawberry on her fork.

"We haven't decided yet," Alyssa said. "Maybe swim some more, watch a video, or I don't know, something. We'll figure it out."

"You'll want to stay out of the sun for the next couple of days," her mom said.

She popped the strawberry in her mouth and chewed. Madison watched, longing to trade her gooey eggs for some fruit. "I have to swing by the studio," Alyssa's mom said. "You girls are welcome to come. I know it would be boring for you, Alyssa, but Madison's never been, and you'll be inside in the air conditioning."

"Aaugh … I don't know," Alyssa said. "Dumb old Swick-the-tick will probably be there and—"

"No," Jessica said, picking up her coffee. "They didn't rehire him for Season Two. Thank heaven."

Alyssa brightened. "Well, that's good. You

won't have to deal with him trying to bother you there."

We should go to the set, Madison thought. *The dog won't be there*. "I think that would be fun," she said.

Alyssa squinted at her. "Really?" Alyssa said.

"Yeah!" Madison said. "Are you kidding me? What kid wouldn't want to see the inside workings of the TV business?"

Alyssa shrugged. "Okay then, but I'm warning you, it's really, *really* boring. It's a lot of sitting around."

Alyssa's mom laughed, low and throaty. "Well, I can't debate you on that, my dear," she said, with a smile in her eyes. "But lord help me, I love it."

"We won't be too long," Alyssa's mom said, as Maximilian wove deftly through the speeding traffic on the freeway. "Just a few hours."

"How come you have to go in?" Alyssa asked. "It's Friday. I thought production didn't start until Monday."

"Since the show has moved to L.A., they've switched to a local crew, so we need to make sure everything matches."

"What's that mean?" Madison asked. She was feeling a bit better. At breakfast she had managed to lift the egg off and set it to the side of her plate without the yolk popping and oozing all over the place. Underneath the egg was a slice of ham and an English muffin, both of which she gobbled up. And then Berta came in with a glass pitcher of that delicious fresh orange juice. When Madison finished the first glass, Berta poured her another, which was even more delicious than the first—although now Madison was questioning the wisdom of downing the two very large glasses of orange juice. She was starting to feel a need-to-pee pressure building in her bladder.

"Well, what it means," Jessica Ashton replied, "is that the wardrobe, hair, and makeup departments are all new. We have the same cinematographer, thank goodness. But we have to do a test run to make sure that the look of the show stays the same. The wardrobe and makeup departments have reviewed the footage we've shot, so they have some idea of the look of the show. Today, they will get me ready, set wardrobe for the first few shows, and then do camera tests and compare them to the footage from last year."

"Oh," Madison said.

Alyssa laughed. "You don't have any idea what she's talking about, do you?"

"No," Madison said, a laugh escaping, which did not help the peeing situation at all. "You're right. No idea whatsoever." She crossed her legs and squeezed. "Um … How long is it until we get there?"

"Depends on traffic," Maximilian said. "If vee keep travelling along zis smoothly, it vill be fifteen, twenty minutes."

Fifteen to twenty minutes. Okay, I can manage that, Madison thought.

"Hey," Alyssa said, flipping open a cabinet that held a little fridge. "Want something to drink? Water? Juice?"

"No thanks," Madison said.

"You like juice," Alyssa said. "We've got apple, cranberry cocktail, and your favourite, orange."

"Um … no, thank you. I'm not … thirsty," Madison said. The need-to-pee pressure was building. She was starting to sweat. "Okay, then," Alyssa said, snagging herself a water, unscrewing the top, and taking a long swig.

Madison wrenched her gaze away from the fluid glugging out of the bottle and down Alyssa's throat and stared out of the window.

Luckily the traffic held, and eighteen sweaty minutes later they arrived at the studio. Madison now had her legs wrapped twice around each other and was trying not to squirm.

There was a uniformed guard at the gate. Max rolled down his window, the hot outside air blasting in. He gave the guard their names. The guard scanned the names on his clipboard, crouched down so he could see into the passenger seat, then smiled. "Nice to see you again, Miss Ashton," he said, tipping his hat. "You'll be going to Stage seven." He filled out a parking pass and handed it to Max. "You know where to go?" he asked Max.

"Sure tink," Max said. "But if you kood gif us vun of your maps for zee younksters here?"

The guard ripped two off his pad and handed them through. "Have a nice time, kids," he said. "Might want to check out what's going on at Stage eleven," he said with a wink. He went into his guardhouse and pressed a button. The barrier lifted, and Max drove over two seriously-*not*-fun-for-Madison's-bladder speed bumps and onto the lot.

Alyssa leaned over and patted Madison's hand. "Don't look so nervous," she whispered. "It's nothing fancy. Only a dumb old studio lot."

"Nothing fancy to you," Madison whispered back. "And I'm *not* nervous."

"Yeah, right. You look like you're ready to jump out of your skin."

Madison opened her mouth to tell Alyssa the reason *why* she was jumpy, but Max glided the car to a stop. There was a skinny guy wearing beat-up jeans, a baggy T-shirt, dark sunglasses, and a baseball cap leaning against the huge beige, windowless building with a large black number 7 painted on it. He was talking into a walkie-talkie, making the few straggly wisps of hair clinging to his chin waggle as he spoke. Alyssa elbowed Madison. "See," she said, eyes twinkling. "Pretty glamorous, huh?" He was probably out of high school, because he had a job and everything, but it was hard to guess his age.

"Are we there?" Madison asked. "Can we get out? Is there a bathroom?"

Maximilian lowered his window. "Excuse me, are you vit *Call Me Night*?" Max called.

"Yup," the guy said, pushing away from the building. "What can I do for you?"

"I haf Miss Ashton in zee car," Max said. "Ver vood you like me to take her?"

Madison tapped Maximilian on the shoulder. "And a bathroom," she whispered, feeling embarrassed but bordering on desperate. "If you could please ask him for a bathroom?"

"And zee kid needs a bathroom," Max said, jerking his thumb over his shoulder.

"Sure, no problem. Hey, Miss Ashton," the guy said, thrusting his hand through the open window and missing Maximilian's face by barely an inch. "Seth Cooper at your service."

Miss Ashton raised her eyebrows.

"Oh, right," Seth said, yanking his hand back out again. "You can't reach. Duh!" His cheeks flushed. "Wait, I didn't mean, duh you. I meant, duh me!"

"Relax, Seth, it's okay. I won't bite," Jessica said.

"It's just you're … well, you're one of my favourite actresses of all time, and I …"—he took a deep breath—"and I'm so honoured to have the chance to work with you."

Madison had to shut her eyes and focus on taking and releasing long, slow breaths through her nose.

"Wow," Alyssa whispered. "You *do* have to go to the bathroom."

"Well, I'm glad you like my work. What's your job on the—"

"Mom," Alyssa cut in. "She's gotta go to the bathroom."

"I'm third AD, assistant director, so you'll be seeing a lot of me, Miss Ashton. Anything you want, anything at all, just let me know, and I'll take care of it."

"Okay," Jessica Ashton said. "Well, it sounds like a bathroom is our first priority."

"Right," Seth turned to Max. "Here, follow me. I'll take you to her trailer." Seth took off at a jog, bringing his walkie-talkie up to his mouth. "Miss Ashton has arrived. However, she has a kid with her that needs to pee, so we are going to swing by the trailer first," Madison heard him say.

Someone answered, but with the noise of the car and the static from the radio, Madison couldn't tell what they said. It was embarrassing that everyone in the world now knew that she had to go to the bathroom bad. But she was relieved too, because it would be *way* worse to have an unfortunate accident at her age!

Seth turned the corner, jogged down the side of the building, and turned the corner again. There were a lot of trailers parked in the back. He sprinted over to a long sleek RV, all chrome and black and grey, with darkened windows. He stepped up and swung open the door.

"Go," Alyssa said, giving her a nudge.

"Go where? What do I do?" Madison asked in a panic.

"Here," Alyssa said, grabbing Madison's hand

and hopping out of the car. "I'll come with you." And as they ran toward the trailer, Alyssa called out in a really loud voice. "Man, I gotta pee bad! My BLADDER is about to BURST!"

"Wha . . . ?" Madison stared, startled, at Alyssa, who just grinned and yanked her up the steps and through the trailer. She pulled open the door to the bathroom and thrust Madison inside.

"Go on," Alyssa said, and shut the bathroom door behind her.

Madison got her shorts down and her butt on the toilet in the nick of time.

Never had a pee felt *so* good!

It was a little embarrassing how long she peed, but she didn't care.

"Okay," Madison said, when she finally finished, washed her hands, and emerged from the bathroom about ten pounds lighter. "Your turn."

"My turn for what?" asked Alyssa, who was sitting at the table flipping through a magazine.

"To . . . uh . . . go to the bathroom?"

"Pfft," Alyssa said. "I don't have to go to the bathroom." She set down the magazine and stood up. "Ready?"

"Well, why did you scream that your bladder wa . . ." Madison trailed off, trying to sort it out.

Alyssa shrugged, her face alive with suppressed laughter.

And then Madison got it. "Oh my god," she laughed, shaking her head. "You are such a wackadoodle."

"Takes one to know one," Alyssa retorted, stepping out of the trailer.

Madison flung her arm around Alyssa's shoulders. "Seriously," Madison said. "You are the best friend *ever*!" And just like that, Madison wasn't homesick anymore. She was glad she came to Los Angeles with Alyssa.

They joined the grownups, who were waiting by the car. They were all wearing sunglasses. *Guess you need them,* Madison thought, blinking in the bright California sun, which seemed more piercing than the Oregon sun. *Maybe that's why all the movie stars wear sunglasses.* Made sense. She could use a pair of sunglasses herself.

Seth led them to a heavy industrial door with a red police light above it. They went through—the heavy steel door swinging shut behind them with a *clunk*—and were plunged into pitch-black darkness. Madison couldn't see a thing except tiny shooting-star specks left over from the bright sun outside.

Everyone else was still moving—she could hear their footsteps and the static buzz from the walkie-talkie. And then she could see again. Not well, but enough to make out Seth holding back a thick black drapery that surrounded the door like a large shower curtain. Beyond that was the sound stage. It was immense. There was the smell of paint and sawdust, and the sound of hammers hitting nails, power drills, and people calling out to one another. It was a beehive of activity. Everyone working, building, lugging equipment—moving fast with purpose.

"They want you first in wardrobe," Seth said. "Then you'll do makeup and hair. Oh, and I almost forgot …" He flipped through the papers on his clipboard. "Here it is." He removed a sealed envelope and handed it to her. "Mr. Swick dropped this by the production office for you."

Alyssa's mom handed it back like it was a hot potato. "I would appreciate it if you would have this letter returned to Mr. Swick, and ask the producers to make it clear that, since he is no longer involved in this production, his trying to prolong contact with me could be grounds for harassment."

"Um … Right." Seth blinked and swallowed hard, his Adam's apple bobbing. "I didn't know he was bothering you. Sorry."

"Don't worry about it. How were you supposed to know?"

"Well, I do now," Seth said, his neck and the

tips of his ears bright red. "Don't you worry. I will go take care of this as soon as you are settled in wardrobe."

"Thanks, Seth. I really appreciate it," Jessica said.

Seth's chest swelled proudly under Jessica Ashton's smile. "Right," he said, giving a quick nod, and then they continued on their journey through the sound stage.

They walked past a living room that had furniture, a fireplace with mementos on the mantel, and pictures on the walls. It was totally complete on the inside, but was missing a wall, and instead of being in a house, it was free-standing. On the other side were just unpainted flats of wood with supports to keep them from falling over. Madison stopped for a second and looked around, breathed it in. The place was a complex mix, a clashing and melding of worlds—practical and magical all mushed together.

"Maddie, you're catching flies," Alyssa said over her shoulder.

Madison snapped her mouth shut and scampered to catch up. A person could get lost in here. "What are those called?" she asked Alyssa, pointing to the large wood flats that were assembled together. There were lots of them. One had painted steps and a railing leading up to a door;

some had windows, others didn't. "Are there hidden rooms in all of them?"

"Mostly," Alyssa said. "They're called sets, and it's where Mom will shoot some of the interior scenes."

"Oh," Madison said, but she didn't know what that was. They wound their way through quite a few more of the sets-things to the far end of the sound stage, went through another door, and started climbing some narrow, worn-down stairs. Madison was glad she wasn't alone. She would never be able to find her way out of this complicated and confusing place.

At the top of the stairs, they went down a long hallway to a double door at the very end. "Here we are," Seth said, opening the door and ushering them into a huge room with light streaming in through large multi-paned industrial windows.

It was an enormous warehouse of clothes, rooms off rooms with racks and racks of clothes—shirts, summer dresses, winter dresses, wool pants, jeans—men's and women's. There were coats and evening gowns on hangers, and piles of clothes on tables, with women sorting through them. Another woman worked at a sewing machine that was whirring away. Some tables were covered with jewellery; another with stacks of hats. There were boots and shoes and purses.

"Tingles," Madison whispered.

"You're so weird," Alyssa said, shaking her head, an affectionate smile on her face.

"It's you who are weird," Madison said, smiling back. "Not knowing how cool this is."

14

a chance meeting

"It's going to be awhile, girls," Jessica Ashton said as she poked her head through the curtain of the makeshift dressing room that had been created in the corner of the wardrobe room. "They've got a ton of clothes in here."

"Oh great," Alyssa groaned. They had been sitting there on hard, metal folding chairs stuck in the corner for quite some time. Alyssa's mom was in the changing room. They could hear voices, and every once in a while, her mom would come out and stand with her arms out while a seamstress crouched at her feet and pinned the hem of the skirt or pants and then stood up and pinned some more along the back, under the arms, and under the breasts. There was a lot of discussion, and sometimes they would have Jessica traipse to wherever the production offices were to do show-and-tell for the producers.

"Honey, why don't I get you some money?" Alyssa's mom said, a slight furrow forming on her forehead. Nothing like the frown lines Madison's mom had on her forehead, but up close, Madison could see the beginnings of them. "And you girls can check out the store."

"I guess," Alyssa said, and sighed. "Might as well."

Alyssa's mom disappeared and returned a second later with her billfold in her hand. She pulled out a hundred-dollar bill and handed it to Alyssa. Madison's eyes widened. She'd never seen a hundred-dollar bill up close before.

"Mom," Alyssa said, shoving it back, her face flushing. "God, why do you do that?"

"Do what?" Alyssa's mom asked, looking confused.

"Do you know how embarrassing it is for a kid my age to walk around with a hundred-dollar bill? It looks like I'm a jerk—either that or a thief!" Alyssa huffed out an angry breath. "Just give us a twenty."

An expression of weariness flashed across Jessica's face and then was gone. "Okay," she said.

"Fine." She put the hundred back in her billfold and pulled out a twenty. "If you find you need more, let me know."

Alyssa had no trouble finding her way downstairs, through the sound stage, and out the door.

"How in the world did you manage that?" Madison asked.

Alyssa shrugged. "Seen one sound stage, you've seen them all. The layout is pretty similar no matter where you go." She pulled the studio map out of the back pocket of her jeans and unfolded it. "Let's see." She squinted at it. "We turn right up ahead, left at Stage four, and then the store should be here," she said, tapping the map with her finger. She tucked the map back in her pocket, and they headed off.

Ten minutes later, they were in the snack section of the store. "I can't decide," Madison said, "between spicy or sweet."

"You can get both," Alyssa said.

Madison shook her head. "I'd feel like I was being too greedy—especially using your mom's money."

"Okay," Alyssa said, plucking the Chile Picante CornNuts out of Madison's hand. "These will be mine and you can get the Mars bar, and we'll share."

"Sure you don't mind?" Madison asked.

"Not at all. I actually think this will be the perfect combination." Alyssa plopped the treats on the counter. "Oh, wait." She held up a finger to the cashier. "Be right back." She spun around and headed toward the gum rack with Madison in her wake. "We should probably get some gum so we won't be breathing dragon breath all over the place. I'm thinking—" Alyssa stopped so abruptly that Madison crashed into her hard.

"Oof!" Madison grunted. "Dang!" She had bitten her tongue. It was throbbing. She could taste blood. Alyssa was gripping Madison's forearm hard, her fingernails digging in. "What the heck, Alyssa?" Madison said. "That hurts." But if anything, Alyssa's grip grew even tighter. Madison's gaze travelled from where Alyssa was clenching her arm up to Alyssa's face. She'd gone extremely pale, and the pupils of her eyes were large and dark.

"Are you okay?" Madison whispered, tucking her head close. There were people all around, and she didn't want to embarrass Alyssa. "Maybe you should sit down and put your head between your knees? We can go to the corner over there. No one will—"

But she didn't finish her sentence because Alyssa did a quick about-face, yanked her down the next aisle over, and pulled her to a crouching position by the coffee mugs. "It's him," Alyssa whispered, jerking her head toward the gum rack.

"Who?" Madison asked, trying to peer through the gap in the stuff on the shelves. All she could see were polished black men's dress shoes and the lower legs of a man's dark-grey business suit.

"My dad," Alyssa whispered.

"What do you mean your dad?" Madison whispered back. "You don't have a da—" Madison slapped a hand over her mouth, aghast. *Did those words just come out of my mouth?* "I mean you have a dad, but not a dad-dad," she amended quickly, but it was too late, the damage was done and Madison felt terrible. It was bad enough that Alyssa's mother had kept the identity of Alyssa's birth dad a secret until the girls had done some sleuthing and Alyssa had worked up her courage to ask some difficult questions of her mom last November. But now, for Madison to blurt out that Alyssa didn't have a dad? She had a dad. She just didn't know him. "I'm sorry," Madison whispered.

"Why be sorry?" Alyssa said, jutting her chin

out and shrugging her shoulders like she didn't care. "It's the truth."

"What I meant was—"

"Let's drop it," Alyssa said, cutting her off.

"Besides," Madison said, starting to feel a little defensive, "if you don't want me to talk about him then you shouldn't have brought him up."

"Oh, excuse me," Alyssa said sarcastically. "I guess I got thrown when I rounded the gum rack and saw my *not-a-dad* dad standing by it."

"What?" Madison squeaked.

"Yeah," Alyssa said, a slightly bitter look on her face. "And now he's over by the counter paying for his gum. Silly me, getting thrown by a little thing like that."

"Are you kidding me?" Madison rose up to try to see, and to figure out what Alyssa was talking about. "You mean the movie star your mom had an—"

"Shhh ..." Alyssa hissed, clamping her hand over Madison's mouth and yanking her back down before she got a good look. Madison did, however, get a glimpse of his famous tousled golden hair.

Under other circumstances, if one of Hollywood's biggest heartthrobs had been in the room, Madison would have stood right back up and gawked to her heart's content. But this was different. Sure, Alyssa was acting all tough and fierce, but Madison could see how shaken she was. So she didn't push Alyssa's hand off. She stayed squatted down with Alyssa's hand over her mouth, both of them keeping an eye on the door until Josh Lowe exited the store, stepped out onto the street, and turned left.

"Are you sure it was him?" Madison asked, straightening up.

"Of course I'm sure. I'm not a complete idiot."

Madison ran to the door and peeked out, just in time to see the back of him disappearing around the corner. "We should follow him."

"We're *not* going to follow him," Alyssa said, inspecting her chipped nail polish and acting as if she hadn't just run into her father that she'd never met before and who didn't even know she existed. But Madison knew that there was a part of Alyssa that did want to follow him, because otherwise she wouldn't have run to the door as well.

"I'm going," Madison said, pushing open the door.

"Madison!" Alyssa called, shifting from foot to foot, standing in the open door. "We have to get our stuff."

“We’ll pick it up later,” Madison called back, as she started to jog down the street. “This is more important.”

Alyssa hesitated, unsure.

“Come on,” Madison said, turning around, jogging backwards. “What can it hurt? I just want to see where he goes. That’s all. I won’t talk to him or approach him. Come on, Allie.” She smiled in what she hoped was an encouraging manner.

“You’re acting crazy,” Alyssa said, with a frown on her face and her hands on her hips.

“I am crazy!” Madison laughed, breaking into an impromptu crazy dance, her arms and legs flying every which way.

“Oh for Pete’s sake ...” Alyssa muttered, a reluctant smile on her face as she sprinted down the steps to join her friend.

“He turned up here,” Madison said. The two girls were running full tilt now. They dashed around the corner.

There was no one. Just beige, windowless sound stages that looked like big warehouses looming on both sides of the treeless, empty, grey street.

A woman on a golf cart glided past a few streets up.

"Where did he go?" Madison said, her head swivelling.

"Maybe you got the street wrong," Alyssa said. She was bent over with her hands on her knees, trying to catch her breath. Madison couldn't see all of her friend's face, but what she could see was a mix of disappointment and relief.

"No," Madison said. "It was definitely this street." She took off again, ran to the next intersection, and looked both ways. There were some big burly guys rolling equipment across the street, but no Josh Lowe. "Dang! Where did he go?"

She started running again. She knew it was futile, because even an Olympic sprinter wouldn't have made it that far in the time it took them to exit the store and run down the road. But still, she ran. Just in case.

When she got to the next intersection, she looked both ways, but he wasn't there. "Great. We lost him," Madison said, to no one, because Alyssa was still standing in the middle of the street back at that first turn.

Madison wiped the sweat off her face with her arm. Her mouth was dry. It was hot like an oven with all that bright California sun blasting down and the concrete street and buildings capturing it, enhancing it, and blasting it back up again. Madison could see actual waves of heat rising off the street. For a moment, looking back at Alyssa she felt like she was in an old Western: At any moment a sheriff was going to come busting out of an old saloon and yell, "Draw!"

"Maddie?" Madison heard Alyssa call. "We better head back. Mom's going to start getting worried."

"Right," Madison said. She shook her head to clear it. The Wild West was gone. It was just her again, in her shorts and T-shirt, sunburned and sweaty, as she slowly headed back toward her friend.

15
more dog drama

"Maddie . . . time to wake up."

"Huh?" Madison murmured, pulling herself from a deep sleep. It was confusing. Where was she? She managed to force her eyelids open. Tired. So tired.

Car. She was in a car. Whose car? It was discombobulating. Alyssa was sitting next to her grinning. Why was Alyssa here, and what was so funny?

Then it all came rushing back in a flash. She was in California, staying with Alyssa and her mom. They had just spent the afternoon at a movie studio and were driving back to the house.

Madison sat upright. How embarrassing. She had fallen asleep in the car like a little kid. She became aware of a little drool that had dribbled from the corner of her mouth. She wiped it quickly. Hopefully nobody had noticed.

The car slowed to a stop. The gates at the top of the driveway opened, and Maximilian eased the car through.

"Too much excitement must have tired you all out," Alyssa's mom said.

Madison nodded. Maybe it was the excitement, or getting used to the heat, or maybe it was the fact that she hadn't slept last night because of the—

Woof . . . woof!

Madison looked out the window and tried to act casual while she tried to tamp down the jolt of adrenaline surging through her. The gigantic Nadine was loping along beside the car, escorting it to the front door of the house with a huge *I'm-hungry-and-want-to-eat-human-flesh* grin on her face.

Max pulled up to the front door. He got out and popped the trunk to get Alyssa's mom's script bag. Alyssa's mom got out. Alyssa got out. Madison didn't.

"Maddie?" Alyssa said, looking at her through the window. "What are you doing?"

"Oh," Madison said, trying to be nonchalant.

"I'm still a bit tired. Think I'll take another little nap before I come inside." She stretched and worked up a passable yawn for good measure.

Alyssa snorted. "Knock it off, Madison."

"You're going to get awfully hot in that car," Alyssa's mom said. "With the engine off, the air conditioning won't—"

"She's not sleepy, Mom," Alyssa said. "She's scared of the dog."

"Of Nadine?" Alyssa's mom looked surprised. "But she's such a cupcake," she said, scratching Nadine behind an ear. Nadine leaned into her and made a moaning sound. "See," she said, turning to Madison. "She's all looks. She wouldn't hurt a flea."

"Unless she didn't like zee flea, then all bets are off," Maximilian said with a wolfish grin.

"But she would like Madison," Alyssa said. "Maddie, you're my friend. Nadine would *never* bite you."

"I know," Madison said. She felt miserable. Everyone was looking at her. And waiting outside in the hot heat for her to stop being so stupid and get out of the car so they could go inside. She took a deep breath, braced herself, and reached for the door handle. She opened the door—her jaw set, her body stiff—and stepped out.

Nadine bounded over and sniffed at her. Madison made herself not run, not move, not squeak. Nadine slurped her tongue across the back of Madison's hand. There was a rushing noise in her ears, and her heart was going *boom ... boom ... boom.*

"See, she likes you," Alyssa was saying.

Madison tried to open her mouth and say something, but no words would come out; they were all caught somewhere in her chest.

"It's really fine, honey. She won't hurt you. See, she's wagging her stump. If she had a tail, it would be swishing back and forth. She's really a friendly dog. She just looks ferocious," Alyssa's mom said. "Go ahead, give her a pet."

She made it sound like Madison had a choice, but she didn't. Everyone was waiting to see if she was a coward or not. Madison forced her hand to rise up and pat the dog's head. "There," she said, putting her hand quickly behind her back. "I did it." She made herself smile. "It was nice. Can we go inside now?"

"Sure," Alyssa's mom said. "You were very brave, Madison."

Moving slow and steady, Madison followed everyone as they headed toward the front door. She tucked her hands in her underarms and walked as close as possible without stepping on the backs of anyone's shoes. This way, if Nadine tried any funny business, everyone would be right there to pull the dog off. It had taken Mr. Eckle a few yanks before he got Mrs. Bachrach's Pomeranian to unclench its jaws. How long would it take to get Nadine to let go? Mrs. Bachrach's Pomeranian could only reach Madison's calves, and that was with jumping. Nadine wouldn't have to jump. She could just plop her front paws on Madison's shoulders and rip out her throat! Madison swallowed hard. *How long does it take for a dog to rip out one's throat?* she wondered, feeling panic rise. She stuffed it down and removed herself from her body, hovering above it like she was a puppeteer handling the strings that made her legs move up and down.

She was trying to appear all calm, but when Nadine butted Madison with her big dog head, her response must not have been as calm as she had hoped. Everyone had stopped in their tracks and was staring at her. "Um ..." Madison said. "It was nothing. I'm okay."

"Then why did you scream?" Alyssa asked.

"I screamed?"

"Yes," Alyssa said, her voice very slow and patient. "You screamed. You went 'AAAAHHHH!'"

"Oh, that," Madison said, trying to laugh it off. "Um … Nadine, well, she, um … bumped me with her head and it, uh …" Nadine head-butted her again. "AAAAHHHH!" Madison shrieked, leaping in the air.

"Yes," Alyssa said, arching an eyebrow and trying not to laugh, "we see. Nice demonstration, Nadine." Nadine wagged her behind, her tongue lolling out the side of her mouth. "You dumb mutt," Alyssa said, her voice full of affection.

Nadine woofed and then head-butted Madison again, who, by biting her lip, managed not to scream this time.

"She just wants you to pet her," Alyssa said. "That's why she's nudging you with her head. She likes you!"

"Uh-huh …" Madison nodded. Her mouth was so dry, all the moisture sucked right out.

"Zee kid's terrified," Max said. "Look at her face. She's vite as a ghost." Max grabbed Nadine's collar. "Hey girl, vhy don't you come hang out vit me?"

"No," Madison said. She was trying to sound firm and in control, but instead her "no" had burst out in a high-pitched squeak. She blew out a lungful of stale air. "I've *got* to get over this," she said. "It's stupid, me being so scared."

"It's how you feel," Alyssa's mom said. "No

need to beat yourself up. We'll just try to keep Nadine out of your way while you're here. And if that doesn't work, maybe we can find a place to board her."

"Mom," Alyssa said, her face worried, "that's not safe for you."

"Alyssa's right," Maximilian said. "Zee security specialist vas kvite clear on zee need not only for a regular patrol and an alarm system but also zee necessity for zee visual and audible presence of a large guard dog."

Madison looked at the concerned faces around her. "I can do this," she said.

"Are you sure about this, honey?" Alyssa's mom asked, looking at her dubiously. "Don't feel like you have to be a superhero. I am sure we will be able to sort something out."

16
old wounds

"Was it weird?" Madison asked.

She and Alyssa were lying on the lawn in the shade of a tree and using Nadine for a pillow. A *pillow!* Madison shook her head and smiled. *Who would have imagined? Too bad Dad couldn't be here to see this!*

The gardener/caretaker/all-purpose-man Fred came up with the idea. He made Nadine lie down and told her to stay. Then asked Madison to pet Nadine. After she got used to placing her hand on Nadine, he had her wrap her arms around the dog and give her a hug. Madison was amazed that she had actually been able to do it. And somehow she had managed the transition from a tentative hug to lying down with her head resting on Nadine. The first five minutes was a sweaty, heart-in-the-mouth experience, but now, she was almost getting used to it. The dog's fur wasn't soft. It was short and bristly, and her body was extremely muscular. Madison could hear grumbling in Nadine's stomach as Madison's head gently rose and fell in rhythm with the dog's warm breath. The sky was clear, with a few unravelled strands of cotton clouds streaked across it. It wasn't as blue as the Oregon sky on account of the smog that coated the sky with a slight brownish-grey haze.

"Was what weird?" Alyssa asked, sitting up and plucking a blade of grass and then lying back down again. Nadine lifted up her head and glanced over. Madison's heart stopped for a beat, but then Nadine just grunted and flopped her head back down. Madison had worried for nothing. She slipped her hand up and patted Nadine's flank. "Good girl," she whispered.

"Was what weird?" Alyssa asked again.

"Huh?" For a second Madison couldn't remember what they were talking about, and then it came back. "I was wondering ... Was it strange for you to bump into Josh Lowe? To see him face to face?" she said. "You knowing he is your dad, but him thinking you're just some kid."

Alyssa shrugged. "The whole situation is weird," she said. Running her thumbnail through the centre of the blade of grass and then placing it between her two thumbs, she blew. A whistle came out, sharp and clear. Nadine got up, tumbling the girls off her. "Nadine," Alyssa admonished, but the dog just nudged Alyssa with her wet nose.

"Yuck," Alyssa said, wiping the trail of dog snot off. Then she blew on the grass again. The whistle caused Nadine to leap sideways in a little hop-dance. The expression on Nadine's face reminded Madison of Scooby-Doo and made Madison laugh—even though she was still a bit nervous around dogs.

"Besides," Alyssa said, "it's not like we had a deep heart-to-heart or anything. He didn't even notice me."

"He must have noticed you," Madison said. "You were standing right there."

"Nope." Alyssa was acting all cheerful and it would have fooled most people, but Madison could see something more was lingering behind her eyes. "Nada. Not even a glance," Alyssa said, all jaunty like a comedian. She flicked the blade of grass off her thumb like she was killing a bug. It flew up in the air and then disappeared in the carpet of grass on the ground. "It was as if I was … invisible." She laughed and wiggled her fingers like a magician, her violet irises almost black from emotion. She blew out an angry puff of air and then flopped on her back, covering her eyes with her arm.

Madison thought of her own dad and how even when he was mad at her for breaking the rules, or was worried about not enough work and how they were going to pay the bills, how *even* then, when he looked at her, she could tell by the softening in his face and the caring in his eyes that he loved her. And that he would do anything for her to have a good life and to keep her safe.

"Alyssa," Madison said, "if he knew you, he would love you."

"You don't know that," Alyssa said. Madison couldn't see her eyes, but it sounded like she might be crying.

"I do know that," Madison said. "He would love you, and he would be proud that you were his daughter."

"What*ever*." Alyssa jumped to her feet, keeping her face turned away from Madison. "I'm going to take a swim," she said, her voice sounding strained.

"Okay," Madison said. If Alyssa didn't want to talk, that was fine. She would when she was ready. "Shall we go change into our swimsuits then?"

"Screw the swimsuits," Alyssa said, stalking across the grass, Nadine trotting beside her. Madison followed, unsure what was next, but not wanting to upset Alyssa further.

They rounded the corner and there was the pool, a sparkling turquoise oasis. Alyssa picked up speed, jogging at first and then breaking into a run. *Oh my goodness,* Madison thought. *I think she's going to …*

SPLOOOSH!

Alyssa had leapt into the pool with all her clothes on!

Um … well … okay, Madison thought. *Here goes …* But she kicked her shoes off before she started running because she didn't have a closetful like Alyssa and couldn't afford to ruin them. "Bombs away!" Madison yelled as she hurled herself up into the air, grabbed her knees, tucked them into her chest, and landed with a big *SPLASH!* in the cool refreshing water beside her best friend.

17
a ghost?

That night, Madison lay in her bed with her eyes closed. *Okay … just relax,* she told herself. *You are home in Rosedale, safe and sound in your nice cozy bed.* She heard the *shhhh* and *whir* of the central air conditioning coming through the vents. *But we don't have air conditioning at home,* the voice inside piped up.

That's not air conditioning, she thought soothingly. *That is Gina, in her bed on her side of the room, breathing her snuffly sleep-breath.*

Humph! Doesn't sound like any kind of Gina snuffle noises I've ever heard.

Madison opened her eyes and sighed. It was no use. She might as well stop fighting the facts. This was going to be another sleepless night. She had eleven more nights to get through before her visit was over. *Is it possible to survive without sleep?*

Bump ... Thunk ...

Oh great, Madison thought, turning onto her side and pulling the covers up over her ears. *Now the house noises start.*

Rattle ... rattle ...

Madison sat upright. *Rattling? Why are the windows rattling? They didn't rattle last night.* And that was when she became aware of the bed vibrating underneath her. "Oh my god ..." she whispered. "There is a ghost ..." She opened her mouth to scream, but before the sound could travel from the pit of her gut through her throat and burst out of her mouth, the connecting door slammed open.

"Madison!" Alyssa shouted. "Earthquake! Get in the doorway!"

"Wha ... Huh?" Madison stammered. "An earthquake?"

"Yes!" Alyssa yelled. "Get in the doorway!"

Madison scrambled out of bed and ran to the bathroom doorway where Alyssa and Nadine were waiting. The room was shaking like an old washing machine.

Then, as quickly as it had started up, the shaking and loud noises stopped.

Alyssa's bedroom door flew open and Alyssa's mom hurried to them, securing her cream-coloured silk robe around her waist. "Are you all right?" she asked, her face concerned. "Weren't too scared?" She pulled them both in for a hug, kissing Alyssa on the top of her head. "It was good thinking to get in the doorway."

"That was Alyssa," Madison said. "I didn't know what was going on."

Alyssa brushed the credit aside. "You were half-asleep. I'm sure you would have figured it out."

"Well," Alyssa's mom said, giving both girls another squeeze. "Let's be grateful it was only a small earthquake and hope we don't have another."

It wasn't until later, when both girls were safely ensconced in Alyssa's bed with Nadine snoring peacefully on the floor beside them, that Madison confessed the truth of the matter.

"You know when you burst into my room?" Madison said.

"Mm … hm," Alyssa replied.

"And you said I was half-asleep and that's why I hadn't figured out we were having an earthquake?"

"Yeah."

"I wasn't half-asleep. I wasn't *any* asleep. I thought the shaking and rattling was …" Madison chuckled. "You aren't going to believe this, but I thought it was a ghost."

"A what?" Alyssa said with a half laugh, flipping onto her side to look at Madison.

"I know!" Madison shook her head, the laughter bubbling up. "I'd been lying there for some time, trying to be brave, but everything is so different here. I'm used to sharing a room with Gina, and your house is so big and makes all these thunking and groaning noises at night, and it kind of freaks me out. So when the bed started shaking, I was sure it was a ghost and—"

Alyssa flipped on the bedside light. She wasn't laughing anymore. "You've been scared?" she asked.

And suddenly it didn't seem so funny to Madison either. She nodded, a thick lump forming in her throat. She nodded, because she didn't trust her voice.

"You should have told me," Alyssa said.

"I …" Madison said, staring down at the bedspread. "I was embarrassed."

"Well, it would be way more fun for you to sleep in here. This bed is huge, and then it would be like one huge gigantic sleepover."

"You sure?" Madison asked, sneaking a peek at Alyssa to see if she meant it.

"Yes!" Alyssa said, giving a little excited bounce. "It would be a million times more fun!"

"Okay, then," Madison said, smiling at her

best friend. "But if you change your mind, or get tired of me sleeping in here, you just have to say the word."

"All right," Alyssa said, sticking out her pinky and latching it onto Madison's. "It's a deal."

18
star tours

"I think we should go to Disneyland. Not tomorrow because Sunday will be pretty crowded, but maybe Monday would be good," Alyssa said as the girls passed each other on their bikes. "What do you think?"

"Sure," Madison called back as she followed the circular driveway around the eucalyptus tree in front. "I would love to do that! I've never been to Disneyland before." They sped past each other again. Alyssa was now entering the circular part of the driveway and Madison was on the straight stretch. Madison balanced out the bike and carefully removed her hands from the handlebars. She was able to go three and a half rotations of the pedals before the bike started to wobble and she had to grab the bars again. Her plan was to return to Rosedale and impress upon Joey Rodriguez that riding with no hands was not just for boys. First though, she had to learn how to do it.

"I know you've never been!" Alyssa yelled, putting on a burst of speed and whizzing past her. "That's why I suggested it. Mom starts shooting on Monday, but I'm sure she wouldn't mind if Maximilian gives us a ride to the Magic Kingdom after he drops her off. She can easily get one of the production drivers to give her a ride home when she's done." Alyssa reached the gates at the end of the driveway and managed the tight turn without having to stop.

"I hope he can," Madison said. "That would be so exciting!"

Alyssa stopped her bike and waited for Madison to turn around and catch up, and then she pushed off again, the two girls riding at a peaceful pace side by side. "Well, don't build it up too much in your mind. Yes, Disneyland is fun, but it's also very crowded. By the end of the day, you'll be exhausted and your feet will feel like they've been stomped on by elephants." They circled the tree pedalling in unison, almost like synchronized swimmers. "And for the best rides, you have to wait in line for a long time."

"How long?"

"Well, it depends on the day. Sometimes

forty-five minutes, but once, I was in line for almost two hours!"

"Two hours standing in line for one ride? Holy cow!"

"And not only that, but the crowds—"

"JESSICA ASHTON!" a disembodied voice bellowed.

Madison looked at Alyssa wide-eyed. "What the heck?" Madison said.

"Oh god," Alyssa groaned. "I hate this guy!" She stood up and pedalled hard, steering the bike off the driveway and onto the lawn where she jumped off, the bike crashing to the ground with a clatter.

"HEY, JESSICA, WHY DON'T YOU COME OUT AND SAY HI TO YOUR FANS?"

"Come on," Alyssa shouted, as she sprinted toward the house.

"WE KNOW YOU ARE IN THERE!" A skinny guy, pimply-faced with long stringy hair, wearing a backwards baseball cap, sunglasses, and skateboarder shorts, appeared at the wrought-iron gates at the top of the drive. He was bellowing into a bullhorn. It was really loud. "OR ARE YOU TOO BUSY, FEATHERING YOUR *LUV* NEST? HEY, MR. SWICKY-BAYBEH, WHY DON'T YOU BOTH COME OUT AND WE'LL TAKE SOME NICE PHOTOS?!" The guy cackled, and then suddenly, he pivoted and his eyes focused like a laser beam on Madison. "Hey, you," the guy said, pointing at Madison, who was still frozen to the spot. "Are you her kid?" His voice was almost gentle. "Come here. I won't hurt you. Just want to chat."

"Maddie," Alyssa yelled. "Don't let them take your picture!"

And it was like the spell was broken. Madison leapt off her bike and ran.

"HEY, EVERYONE!" she heard the guy bawl. "GET OUT OF THE BUS! WE'VE GOT OURSELVES A GENUINE TV STAR'S KID RIGHT HERE ON JESSICA ASHTON'S PRIVATE DRIVE!"

This must be how the wildebeest feels when the hyenas are closing in, she thought, her legs pumping as fast as they could.

Just as she was turning the corner of the house, she saw a swarm of tourists piling off the Star Tours shuttle bus with cameras and cell phones at the ready. But she was safe now. She was out of their view, beside her friend and bent over at the waist trying to suck in air. "That's craziness," Madison panted.

"WHOOPS!" She heard the guy hoot. "YOU COMPADRES WERE TOO SLOW ON THE DRAW. SHE'S GONE, BUT DON'T WEEP.

ALL IS NOT LOST. HER BIKE'S STILL IN THE DRIVE. YOU CAN GET A GENUINE PICTURE OF A REAL LIVE MOVIE STAR'S DAUGHTER'S BIKE!"

"That guy is nuts!"

"Yeah," Alyssa said. "I hate all the tour buses coming by. It's bad enough they stop and take pictures like we're monkeys in the zoo, but he's the worst. Him with his stupid bullhorn. I'd like to cram the dumb thing down his throat!"

"They don't all carry them?" Madison asked.

"No." Alyssa snorted in disgust. "Only him. The jerk."

"HEY, KID!" They could hear him bleating. "WE AREN'T LEAVING. SO YOU MIGHT AS WELL COME BACK AND TAKE A FEW PICTURES WITH MY COMPADRES. HOW 'BOUT IT? HUH? I'LL GIVE YOU FIVE BUCKS!"

Alyssa pushed off the wall. "You ready?" she asked. Madison straightened up and nodded.

"HOW 'BOUT FIVE BUCKS AAAAND … THE REST OF MY SLURPEE?"

They walked around the back of the house to where Nadine was lying peacefully on the breakfast room floor by the door, soaking up the sun.

"IT'S CHERRRRRY!"

Alyssa opened the door. "Nadine," she said,

her right arm sweeping outwards, her finger pointing in the direction of the gate. "*Watch* him!"

Nadine transformed in an instant from a peaceful, sleeping pet to a ferocious guard dog. She leapt to her feet, all bristling fur and lips pulled back to bare teeth. *"RRRAAAAHHHGGG!"* she snarled, as she raced out the door and rounded the house, deep bone-rattling barks erupting from her belly.

"Wow," Madison said, once she found her voice. "That was … uh … impressive."

Alyssa smiled, daintily dusting off her hands. "Shall we?"

The girls stepped inside, enveloped once again in the cool air-conditioned house, and shut the door behind them.

"Ahhhh …" Alyssa said, her face relaxing.

Berta was in the kitchen. "*Le gustaría un poco de limonada?*"

"*Sí, gracias,*" Alyssa replied.

Berta got a pitcher of lemonade from the fridge and poured some into two tall glasses with ice.

"*Gracias,*" Madison said shyly. Berta beamed.

They sat down on the stools by the counter and watched Berta sprinkle a handful of flour and then roll out some dough. Madison took a large sip from her glass, the ice cubes clinking, the lemonade refreshing and tart with just the right amount of sweetness. She could hear the muffled sounds of Nadine's frenzied barking out at the gate, the commotion of everyone running for the bus, and the Star Tours shuttle bus peeling out of the driveway. It was wrong that people could harass Alyssa and her mom like that. It wasn't right. The obnoxious guy with the bullhorn thought he was being funny, but he wasn't. He was being rude.

Madison took another long drink from her glass. *It's not fair,* she thought. *Someone needs to teach that guy a lesson.*

19

the best idea EVER!

Alyssa was asleep. It hadn't taken her long—five, ten minutes tops. She looked different when she was asleep. Her face seemed younger with all the tension drained out. Her mouth was open slightly, her eyelids fluttering. Must be dreaming.

Madison wasn't sleeping, but it wasn't because she was scared of Nadine or the house noises anymore. She wasn't. Which was sort of an odd feeling, because she had been so scared before. But she was finding that having Nadine by the bed was a surprisingly comforting and cozy feeling. She reached down and petted Nadine's head. Nadine, half-asleep, tilted her head up a bit so Madison could scratch behind her ears.

The dog's fur was still wet. Madison chuckled under her breath, remembering Nadine's surprised indignation. They had let her outside for one last pee before bed, and Nadine was taking her sweet time, smelling each bush and each blade of grass, trying to decide which plants she should honour with her urine.

"Nadine, stop stalling!" Alyssa had yelled from the doorway. Nadine had looked over at them and then put her nose down to track another interesting smell through the grass ... And that's when the automated sprinkler system had gone on. The look on Nadine's face when she got squirted in the butt with that water! She yipped and levitated a good foot in the air.

Madison laughed again, just thinking about it.

"Everything okay?" Alyssa mumbled sleepily.

"Yes, everything's fine," Madison whispered. "Sorry. Go back to sleep."

"Okay," Alyssa yawned. She rolled onto her side and was asleep again.

I wish I was an expert sleeper like that, Madison thought. And then her mind turned to the day: the promise of Disneyland, riding the bikes, the jerk with the bullhorn. *Stupid creep!* She gave Nadine another generous scratch behind her wet ears—and suddenly she got the most *brilliant* idea in the *whole* world!

20
smelly jelly

"I would like a bottle of your smelliest Smelly Jelly Sticky Liquid, please," Madison said.

"My smelliest?" the sales clerk said, his brow furrowing as he peered at her over the top of his bifocals. "Well, that would be difficult to say. They are all pretty smelly—hence the name." The sales clerk rounded the counter of the fishing goods store and headed down an aisle. "I think it's down this aisle. It's been awhile since anyone's requested it," he said.

"Smelly Jelly Liquid?" Alyssa asked. "What's that for?"

"You put it on your worms, jigs, hard baits, soft plastic lures," the sales clerk replied over his shoulder. "Doesn't matter what. You use it, and you are pretty much guaranteed to catch your limit. The fish go nuts for it. They smell it and bite down and don't let go."

Alyssa looked at Madison, a dubious expression on her face. "You want to go *fishing*?" she asked, wrinkling her nose.

Madison rubbed her hands together and hunched over like an evil witch. "All will be revealed, my dear," she cackled softly. "All will be revealed." She spun around and followed the sales clerk before Alyssa could ask any more questions. She wanted to have all the ingredients in place before she revealed her amazingly brilliant plan to Alyssa.

The sales clerk stopped. "Here we are," he said, bending over and peering at the lined-up bottles. "We've got shrimp, sardine, anchovy … Oh, and here is my personal favourite: crawfish. I find the Crawfish Smelly Jelly Sticky Liquid to be especially pungent."

"Oh yeah, I remember Crawfish! That's one of my grandpa's favourites," she said, pulling out a bottle. "It is truly toxic." Gleeful laughter threatened, but she held it back and tried to keep her face neutral; she didn't want this nice old guy to know what she intended to use the *especially* pungent Crawfish Smelly Jelly Sticky Liquid for. He might be a stickler and refuse to let her buy it.

They went to the counter and he rang it up. Madison paid the five dollars and seventy-nine cents. Including Madison's purchase at the previous store, this venture had cost Madison most of her spending money. *But it is money well spent,* Madison thought with a grin. *Because my plan is truly brilliant!*

"Good luck with the fish," the old guy said, handing her the receipt and her change. "Not that you'll need it. That Smelly Jelly works like a charm. Be careful how you handle it. You don't want to spill it on yourself, because that stuff is really stinky and takes a bit of effort to wash off."

And that did it. Madison couldn't help herself. A snort of laughter escaped. "Thank you," she managed to squeak. "Come on!" She grabbed the bag containing the Smelly Jelly with one hand and Alyssa's arm with the other and fled the store before she lost it completely.

"What is going on?" Alyssa demanded, after they slid into the back seat of the car and Madison dissolved into laughter.

Madison was tempted to tell Alyssa, but she could see Maximilian watching them in the rear-view mirror. "I'll tell you when we get home," Madison managed to get out amid helpless snorts of laughter. "But trust me, Alyssa, you are going to *love* it."

21
the reveal

"Are you ready?" Madison asked, her eyes twinkling.

"Yes," Alyssa said, nodding her head.

The girls were sitting cross-legged on their bed. Madison's purchases, still in their plastic bags, lay on the duvet between them.

"Are ... you ... sure?" Madison said slowly, extending, savouring the moment before the big reveal.

"I am *dying* of curiosity, Maddie. You've got to tell me now, before I burst!"

"All right." Madison plunged her hand into the beige plastic bag from the fishing goods store. "Crawfish Smelly Jelly Sticky Liquid," she said, pulling it out of the bag with a flourish. "We have to be super careful with this." She unscrewed the top. "We do *not* want it to spill." She lifted the cap from the bottle. It took less than a second for the stink to hit their nostrils.

"Whoa!" Alyssa said, reeling backwards and clutching her nose. "What the heck is that?" Her eyes were literally bugging out of her head "And why did you think it would be a good idea to bring it into our room?!"

Madison cackled as Alyssa ran to the window like a woman drowning and wrenched it wide open.

Nadine, unfortunately, was *very* interested in the fishy stink. She tried to climb onto the bed, which she was totally *not* allowed to do. "*No*, Nadine! *Down*!" Madison said in the strict, no-nonsense voice that she had learned to employ when Nadine was misbehaving.

Nadine got a sheepish expression on her face, but she got down, albeit reluctantly, licking her lips and twitching her nose in sniff-overdrive.

Madison slapped the lid back on the bottle and screwed it on nice and tight. "Stinks, huh?" she said to Alyssa, almost beside herself with glee.

"I'll say," Alyssa retorted, still standing by the open window waving her hand frantically in front of her nose and sucking in huge gulps of air. "And that is a good thing because?"

"Because in some cases, hard-to-wash-out

stench is good!" Madison said, triumphantly dumping the two pump-handle Super Soakers out of the other bag and onto the bed.

"What?" Alyssa looked at her with a mixture of bemusement and concern.

"Remember that guy?"

"What guy?"

"The obnoxious one with the bullhorn."

Alyssa groaned. "Maddie, why do you have to ruin a perfectly good day?"

"Well,"—Madison grabbed one of the Super Soakers—"you will never have to worry about him again!" she said, leaping up and hitting a pose, the bed bouncing slightly under her feet. "Because once we fill these puppies"—she waved the pump-action Super Soaker—"with our special mixture of ice water and 'particularly pungent' Crawfish Smelly Jelly, which you have observed is *really* smelly, that guy is going to decide that there are better celebrities to fry!"

"Oh ... my ... god, Maddie!" Alyssa said, her hand flying up to cover the radiant smile that spread across her face. "You are brilliant!" Alyssa flew across the room, jumped on the bed, and grabbed her best friend in a fierce hug. "You are a genius! Can you imagine his face when that stuff hits him?"

"And he won't be able to wash it off!"

"And if he has a date that night . . ." Alyssa said, excited laughter tumbling out as she bounced on the bed.

"She'll go ... sniff ... sniff ... what is that stench?" Madison chortled, bouncing up and down too, like they were on a trampoline. "He'll be sooo embarrassed. He'll never want to come near here again!"

The girls laughed so hard over that vision that they had to fall down and clutch their sore tummies and massage their aching cheeks.

The rest of the afternoon was spent making plans. They combed the property until they found the perfect spot from which to carry out their mission: the large knobby tree whose thick branches hung over the seven-foot-high grey wall that surrounded the exterior of the property. Then they did a few practice runs with water to make sure they could hit their target from up in the foliage of the tree. They figured out that if they tilted the Super Soakers up in the air, they could increase their range from twenty feet to thirty-five feet on a good shot. Not that it was necessary; from their perch in the tree, the front gate wasn't more than ten to twelve feet away tops. And every once in a while, one of them would say, in a refined sort of voice, "particularly pungent"—which would send them off in another bellyaching fit of laughter.

Once they had practiced and reached a level of accuracy that would make a sharp-shooter green with envy, they returned to their bathroom and filled the Super Soakers with their special mixture of water and Crawfish Smelly Jelly Sticky Liquid. Stashing them in the spare fridge in the garage would keep the contents "nice and cold." They were very careful, but still, a little bit of Smelly Jelly got on their hands. They scrubbed and scrubbed with soap and water, but when dinner rolled around, Alyssa's mother's nose went *sniff* ... *sniff* ... and then she said, with her nostrils flaring upwards, "What is that awful smell?"

22
popcorn

"You want to know what gets me?" Alyssa said, pulling off the large purple bow and ripping open the clear cellophane wrapping that enclosed the contents and large wicker basket sitting on the kitchen table. "These *gift baskets* that are always arriving for my mom look *so* exciting, when really, they are just stuffed with junk." Alyssa removed a packet of black pasta. "*Squid ink* pasta?" she read. "See what I mean? Yuck." She plopped it on the table with a grimace and pulled another couple of items out. "*Black Truffle–Infused Olive Oil*—whatever that is? *Gluten-, Sugar-, and Wheat-Free Ginger Molasses Cookies*. Ewww. How could these *possibly* be tasty?" Alyssa set them on the table and took out another package. "*Wabash Valley Farms Amish Country Gourmet Purple Popping Corn.*" Alyssa snorted. "Well, the name is fancy and purple popcorn might be cool in theory, but a bag of un-popped popcorn? How are we supposed to eat that?"

"We could pop it," Madison said, picking up the bag.

"Maddie," Alyssa said, shaking her head. "That isn't microwave popcorn. We can't just dump a bunch in the microwave and turn it on. It's more complicated than that."

"Not really," Madison said, turning the bag over in her hand. "Making popcorn is pretty simple. We just need a pot with a lid, a bit of oil, and some butter—"

"Wait a minute!" Alyssa cut in. "You *know* how to make homemade popcorn?"

Madison glanced up. Alyssa was staring at her like Madison had just announced she had an invisibility cloak. Madison shrugged. "Sure. It's no big deal."

"Who taught you how?"

"My dad," Madison said. She looked back at the bag in her hand. "I've never made this kind, though. I wonder if it's purple when it's popped?"

"Let's try it out!" Alyssa said. "We've got popcorn. I know there's butter in the fridge. What kind of oil do you use?"

"I don't know." Madison shrugged. "Whatever is in the house."

"Well," Alyssa said, plucking the small can of *Black Truffle–Infused Olive Oil* off the table. "Do you think this would work?"

"I don't see why not," Madison said. She opened the lid and took a sniff. "Hmm . . ." she said. "Smells interesting, kind of mushroomy. What do you think?" She held the can under Alyssa's nose.

"I kind of like it," Alyssa said.

"Me too. Now, we need a medium pot with a lid."

Alyssa did a happy twirling dance while she pulled open drawers and cupboards until she found the one containing pots and pans. "This is going to be fun!"

Madison showed Alyssa how to pour a dollop of oil in the pot and how to slide the popcorn around the pot until all the kernels had a thin coating of oil. She had Alyssa turn the burner on, a little bit higher than medium heat. She showed her how to give the pot a good shake every fifteen seconds or so to move the popcorn around so it wouldn't burn—and told her to be sure to keep a hand on the lid when shaking the pot so the lid wouldn't fly off.

As Madison was teaching Alyssa, she felt that her dad was there too. Memories of him showing her so many things flew through her head: how to pop popcorn; how to ride a bike; how to fold her own clothes; how to suck the sweet nectar from the base of a honeysuckle blossom.

Madison glanced over at her best friend, who was staring intently through the glass lid of the pot, her face aglow, her cheeks flushed. Madison felt a wave of sorrow for her friend. It wasn't fair. Alyssa should have those kinds of memories with her dad.

"I can see the oil sizzling around the popcorn kernels!" Alyssa said. And then "Oh!" as she jumped back startled. "It popped!"

"Well, that answers that," Madison said, peering at the fluffy white popcorn morsel that was resting amongst the un-popped kernels. "It's not going to be purple. Give the pot a good shake."

Alyssa did and another kernel popped and another, the popping picking up speed until the pot was almost full, and Alyssa had to take off the lid and pour some of the popcorn out into the waiting colander. "Aaaah!" Alyssa shrieked as several kernels popped and shot across the kitchen. "Help!"

"Don't worry," Madison laughed. "That always happens. When my dad first taught me, a lot more escaped. You're doing great!"

Madison was there in the kitchen with Alyssa,

but she was also thinking about running into Josh Lowe the day before yesterday. The more she thought about it, the more she was convinced it was a sign.

Once the popcorn was popped and Alyssa was melting the butter in the warm pot, the feeling had gotten too big for Madison to ignore. "I think," Madison said, "we should skip Disneyland tomorrow."

"What?" Alyssa said, swirling the butter around to make it melt faster. "I thought you wanted to go."

"I did. I do." Madison wasn't sure how to phrase it, but she knew what she had to say was right. "But I think we should go to the studio with your mom tomorrow instead," Madison said, sliding a dinner plate under the colander to catch any butter drips.

"Why?"

"Disneyland is not going anywhere, but your dad might. He was at the studio Friday—"

"Yeah, I noticed," Alyssa said, picking up a fork and jabbing at the butter. "I was there, remember?"

"Well, I was thinking, he *might* still be there Monday. We should check it out. Just in case. I think it was a sign!"

"It was a coincidence," Alyssa muttered.

"A *sign*," Madison repeated firmly. "What are the chances, out of all the places in the whole wide world, that the two of you would end up in the same store on the same studio lot at the exact same time?"

"Seeing as how he's an actor and my mom's an actor and we are in Hollywood, pretty good."

"Have you ever run into him before?" Madison asked, reaching over and switching off the burner.

"No," Alyssa sniffed with pretend unconcern.

"And ... you're ... how old?"

"Maddie, you know how old I am."

"Eleven," Madison said. "You are eleven years old, and not once in eleven years have you run into your dad."

"Maybe I did," Alyssa said, suddenly very involved in scraping the last bits of old purple polish off her thumbnail. "We could have crossed paths and I just didn't know it."

"I'd buy that," Madison said, looking at Alyssa sternly, "if your father wasn't one of the most famous heartthrobs of all time. There is no way anyone could cross paths with him and not know it."

"You didn't know it was him."

"I was behind you, Alyssa. If I had been in front of you, I would have seen him and known it was him. Good grief, we are talking about *Josh Lowe*. Anyway, we are wasting our breath on quibbling details."

"Quibbling?" Alyssa laughed.

"Quibbling: an unimportant objection or criticism." Madison gestured toward the popcorn. "The butter is melted. You can drizzle it on."

"Right." Alyssa picked up the pot and tipped it slightly so the butter started to pour out in a thin stream over the popcorn. "Like this?"

"Perfect," Madison said. "Make sure you keep the pot moving so the butter is evenly spread. Nice." Madison got the salt shaker from the kitchen table. "And now you toss it and salt to taste."

"Toss it?" Alyssa's eyes widened. The surprised expression on her face was priceless.

Madison laughed. "No, not in the air. It's a cooking phrase, I guess. It means you're supposed to mix it lightly. You know, like 'toss the salad.'"

"Oh," Alyssa said with a nod. She added some salt, mixed the popcorn, tasted, added a bit more salt, stirred it again, took another taste, and smiled. "Yum!" Alyssa looked very pleased with herself. "This tastes *so* good! Wow. I'm never going to make microwave popcorn again." She held the colander of freshly popped, buttery popcorn out to Madison. "Try it," Alyssa said, kind of proud and kind of shy.

They brought the popcorn into the living room and started setting up the Ticket to Ride board game. "About my father," Alyssa said, shuffling the route cards. "Yes, he was at the studio Friday, but that doesn't mean he'll be there tomorrow. And besides, what about my mom?"

"What about your mom?" Madison asked, taking the zip-lock plastic bag of little blue trains out of the box.

"Maybe it would hurt her feelings, me looking for my dad. Make her feel like she's not enough."

"Why would it hurt her feelings?" Madison asked, undoing the bag and dumping the contents out on the table. "It's natural to be curious. He's half of you."

Alyssa didn't answer. Madison could tell she was nervous, but she could see a glimmer of cautious hope in her friend's eyes as well.

"Look," Madison said, "you don't have to decide today whether you want to approach him or anything. We'll do a little sleuthing is all. I know it's a long shot, Alyssa. It is a big studio and it's doubtful we'll find him, but I just think we should—"

"Wait a minute!" Alyssa said, straightening suddenly. "Maddie, do you remember when we arrived at the front gate of the studio and the guard winked and mentioned about something exciting going on at Stage eleven?"

Madison nodded slowly. "Yeah. And?"

Alyssa slapped the route cards on the coffee table, stood up, and started pacing nervously. "Okay. I don't know why I didn't think of it before, but Stage eleven was down that road where we lost him. I bet that's where he's shooting!"

Madison shot to her feet. "You're a genius, Alyssa! I bet you're right. Do you remember where we put that map the guard gave us?"

Alyssa sat down on the sofa, a slightly dazed expression on her face, like she had just gotten off a merry-go-round that was spinning too fast. "We don't need it," she said, her voice barely there. "I saw the number eleven on the building as we ran past."

Madison sat down next to her. Neither one spoke for a minute.

"Do you really think your mom would be upset?" Madison asked.

"I don't know," Alyssa answered.

"When she told you about him last November, did she tell you not to contact him?"

Alyssa shook her head.

"Well," Madison said, "maybe she wouldn't mind?"

They sat a moment longer in the silent living room.

"We should skip Disneyland and go to the studio tomorrow," Madison said. "Yes, we could be wrong. And yes, maybe he's not working at Stage eleven, or maybe he's finished shooting and won't be there. But if he is, it's the chance of a lifetime, and I think you owe it to yourself to check it out."

Alyssa took a breath, held it for a second, and then let it out. "Okay," she said.

23
looking for josh

"Okay," Madison said, popping the last bite of her breakfast burrito in her mouth. "Your mom is on set, we have eaten breakfast . . ."—she wiped her fingers with a napkin and tossed it in the large grey garbage can outside of the craft service truck—"Are you ready to head out?" Madison asked.

"Um . . ." Alyssa looked a little scared. "I have to wash my hands first."

"Your hands?" Madison raised an eyebrow.

"Yes," Alyssa said, a trifle defensively. "My hands. In case we find him and talk to him, I'd rather not do it smelling like breakfast burritos."

"Okay," Madison said. "Let's wash our hands." Alyssa could procrastinate all she wanted, but sooner or later, she and Madison were going to check out Stage 11.

They went back to Jessica's trailer. They washed their hands. They dried them. They rubbed on some of Jessica's hand lotion that smelled like lemons and grapefruit. They were almost out the door when Alyssa thought she might need to use the toilet. Madison waited for her on the sofa. Alyssa was in the bathroom for awhile. When she came out, it was clear that she had not only used the toilet but also had dabbed on some of her mom's clear lip gloss and brushed her hair until it resembled a silky, golden gleaming waterfall.

"You look pretty," Madison said, as they headed out the door.

"Do you think?" Alyssa said, an anxious note in her voice.

"I know," Madison replied firmly.

They didn't talk again until they had passed the store and rounded the corner.

There it was: Stage 11. The place was bustling. Grips were hauling big pieces of equipment, lights, and cables. An assistant director on a walkie-talkie was herding a large group of men and women wearing suits and shiny shoes with sensible heels in through a side door.

"Extras," Alyssa whispered. "Too bad there aren't kids, or we could have tried to blend in. No one would have noticed a couple more extras."

"Yeah." Madison nodded, even though she wasn't sure what an "extra" was. There were so many movie terms and new word meanings.

Alyssa took a deep breath and let it out. "Okay," she said, straightening her shoulders and turning to face Madison, "I'm ready. What's the plan?"

"Um ..." Madison felt her face flush. She didn't really have a "plan." She hadn't thought past finding their way back to Stage 11. "Let's go in," she said.

Alyssa shook her head. "You can't just walk onto someone else's set without an invitation."

"Why not?"

"There are rules. We'd probably get kicked out and—"

Arf!

Madison stiffened, her body instantly going into fight-or-flight mode. She whirled toward the sound.

"Awww ..." Alyssa cooed. "How adorable! Would you look at that?" A grey-and-beige German Shepherd puppy with black-and-white patches was frolicking at the end of a leash that was held by a less-than-enthusiastic production assistant.

"Come on, Gus, pee, for crying out loud," the PA grumbled.

"Is he yours?" Alyssa asked, stepping toward them.

"No," the PA said. "I've been walking him for fifteen minutes, and the dang dog still hasn't gone to the bathroom." Of course, the puppy chose that moment to hunker down and deposit a steaming brown gift on the ground. "Great," he groused. "I was asked to pee the dog. Nobody said anything about poo. Man, that stinks." He gave a tug on the leash. "Come on, Gus. Let's go."

"You have to pick it up," Alyssa said.

"What?" the PA said.

"The poop," Alyssa said. "You are supposed to pick it up. Someone might step in it."

"I'm not picking that up," he said, recoiling. "Are you nuts?"

"It's the law," Alyssa said, crossing her arms. "Don't you have a doggie bag?"

"A what?"

"A doggie bag." The guy looked at Alyssa blankly. "A plastic bag that you scoop it up with. Any plastic bag will do."

"Sheesh," the guy said, rolling his eyes. "I don't believe this."

"Do you want us to hold the puppy while you get one?" Alyssa offered.

"Fine,"—the PA shoved the leash in her hands—"be my guest." He stalked toward a garbage can on the corner, rummaged around, and fished out a plastic bag.

"Oh my," Alyssa said, crouching down and snuggling with the puppy, who was covering her face with enthusiastic licks. "Aren't you the sweetest thing? Maddie, you've got to come pet him. His fur is so soft. Way softer than Nadine's."

But Madison kept her distance. Nadine was all right. She was a sweet dog, but this little squirming puppy was unknown—and its sharp little teeth were tugging on the corner of Alyssa's shirt.

The PA wrapped his hand in the plastic bag, squatted down, and picked up the poop. "My parents," he said, shaking his head, "did not pay for four years at NYU for this."

He tied the bag closed, jogged over to the garbage, and tossed the poop bag in. He came back and took the leash from Alyssa. "Thanks, kid," he said, and away he went, with the floppy-limbed puppy, Gus, bounding behind him.

"You should have petted him," Alyssa said. "He was so soft."

"Next time," Madison said.

They waited by the door for a long time. A lot of people came and went, but no Josh Lowe.

"There are lots of doors on a sound stage, you know," Alyssa said, bumping her back softly against the wall. "He might be using another one."

"Well, tomorrow we'll watch a different one." When they had first arrived, there was a cool breeze blowing, but that was long gone. It was hot. Madison was sweaty. She was longing for a nice cold drink of water.

"I think we should go," Alyssa said. "Mom will be getting worried."

"We can't go yet. We haven't seen him."

"Well, we might not see him, Maddie. And besides, even if we do, what do we do then?"

Madison pushed away from the building. "I'm going inside," she said.

"You're crazy," Alyssa said. "They'll kick you out."

"Maybe they will," Madison said, striding toward the door with more bravery than she felt. "But maybe they won't. And even if they do, so what?" She closed her hand around the metal handle of the door.

"Wait for me!" Alyssa called, running to catch up.

Madison felt a wave of relief rush through her. She was glad that she wasn't going to have to enter alone.

"Here we go," Madison said to her friend as she pulled the door open.

They stepped inside. It was a hubbub of activity. The energy of the place was similar to Alyssa's mom's set, with people shouting and rushing by, everyone seeming to have a place to go, a job to tend to.

"Hey!" A man's voice barked. "What are you kids doing here? This is a closed set!"

Madison looked in the direction of the voice. A tall man with a beard was headed their way with a scowl on his face.

"Sorry," Alyssa squeaked. "Wrong set." She grabbed Madison's arm and yanked her out the door. "Run!" she said.

They ran. They ran and ran until they were safely back in Alyssa's mom's trailer.

24
still trying

It was Friday and Madison was starting to panic. She and Alyssa had continued to go with Alyssa's mother to the studio every morning. And every night they returned home disappointed.

There was a tap on the trailer door. Jessica sauntered over. "Yes?" she said, opening the door and glancing out.

It was Seth, as usual. "Makeup and hair would like to see you for a touch-up, and then I'll walk you onto set."

"All right. Be out in a sec."

"Also," Seth said, his chest puffing up slightly. "I wanted to let you know, I caught Ted Swick trying to sneak into the sound stage. So, I grabbed two of the grips, Big Joe and Johnny, and we *escorted* Mr. Swick off the lot." Seth cleared his throat, looking quite pleased with himself.

"None too gently, I might add. Big Joe had a few *words* with him. I don't think he'll be bothering you in the future."

"Seth, you are such a sweetheart. Thank you so much," Jessica said. She grabbed her script, where she had highlighted her lines in yellow and scribbled notes in black ink in the margin. "And girls, I really appreciate your running lines with me. It was a big help."

"I enjoyed it," Madison said. "It was interesting." She was trying to act all normal, like *yeah, I'm on a TV set in a famous actress's trailer helping her run lines, no biggie*, but it was. Madison didn't know why it felt different than when they were at home, but it weirdly did. When Alyssa's mom was at work and wearing her wardrobe and all done up with fancy jewellery and makeup and hair, it made Madison feel a little awkward and shy. It was almost like the famous Miss Ashton was a completely different person than Alyssa's mom. She had a different kind of energy. Moved differently. Walked differently. Spoke differently. It was like the light inside of her shifted and shone brighter and sometimes darker than the calm, peaceful Alyssa's mom at home.

Yesterday, Madison mentioned it to Alyssa when her mom was on set and they were in her trailer by themselves. Alyssa laughed and brushed it off. "You get used to it," Alyssa said. "Deep down, Mom is still herself, but she's not too. It's like someone else has climbed into her skin and occupies her for awhile."

"Doesn't it freak you out?" Madison asked, because she didn't think she could take it if she came home from school and her parents or grandparents were being someone else.

"No," Alyssa said with a shrug. "It's just her characters rubbing off on her a bit. A week or two after she completes the shooting of a show, she's right back to normal."

But Madison was glad she wasn't Alyssa. She didn't think she would ever be able to get used to it.

Jessica paused at the trailer door, her arm slung up against the frame like she was basking in the sun. "You girls going to come to set or hang out here for awhile?"

Madison snuck a quick peek at Alyssa. "Um … I would like to take another walk first. Stretch my legs a bit," Madison said.

Jessica laughed. "Boy, you are quite the exercise fiend, aren't you? The other big surprise is you and Alyssa coming to set every day this week." Jessica shook her head. "I don't know what's in the Kool-Aid, but please keep drinking it." She smiled at her daughter. "It's such a treat to have you here, honey."

Alyssa flushed and looked a little guilty.

"It's okay, isn't it?" Madison asked. "You won't get in trouble because we like to tromp around the studio lot so much?"

"No, of course not. Just don't get lost. If you guys get hungry, you can grab something at the craft service truck. You remember where it is?" The girls nodded. "Good. Lunch break is set for 3:40. I probably won't be back to the trailer before then."

"We'll see you at lunch then, Mom," Alyssa said. "All right," Jessica said, and then she was gone, the door clattering shut behind her.

"Ready?" Madison said, getting to her feet.

"It's a lost cause, Maddie," Alyssa said, reluctantly rising to her feet. "We've already wasted four whole days trying to track him down and still … nada! You have to go home soon, and after that, who knows when we'll get to see each other again?"

Madison felt a pang in her chest. "We can't do anything about that," she said. "It's just the way things are. But we *can* try to see your dad. We are here. We are going to do this thing."

"What if we run into that grouchy man with

the beard again? He'll remember us, Maddie."

"Then we'll zip out that door and sneak in through a different one," Madison said as she headed for the door. Alyssa followed. Madison knew she had to be the one who propelled this quest forward, because Alyssa was too emotionally involved to admit how important this was to her.

The girls exited the trailer and started the familiar route to Stage 11. "Maybe we haven't spoken to your father yet," Madison said, "but look at all the progress we've made. We now know that the movie he's working on is called *Plummet*. We have confirmed that the interiors are being filmed in Stage eleven. We have discovered that the only reason we haven't bumped into him is because they were out shooting on location Monday, Tuesday, and Wednesday."

"And what is the excuse for Thursday? Jimmy at the gate said the Josh Lowe movie was back on the lot yesterday, and we didn't see hide nor hair of him."

"That is true, but I think we were lurking across from the wrong door. We have to be more aggressive." They were moving past the store now. "We now know where they have the honey wagons parked. We'll linger there. He has to go in and out of his trailer and the makeup trailer and such. This is the day!" Madison reached over and smoothed a strand of Alyssa's hair that was sticking up funny. "Do you know what you want to say?"

"No, I don't." Alyssa scowled. "And I feel like one of my mom's weirdo stalkers."

"You aren't a stalker," Madison said. "You are his daughter, for crying out loud."

"Big whoop," Alyssa said, whirling her pointing finger in the air. "Like he even cares." They turned the corner.

"He doesn't know!" Madison burst out, coming to a halt—wanting to shake her friend by the shoulders. "If he knew, he would—" But Alyssa wasn't looking at her. She was staring wide-eyed over Madison's shoulder. "What?" Madison whirled around. "Oh no ..."

The wardrobe trailer, the makeup trailer, the props truck, the honey wagons were gone. It was just an empty street.

"Maybe they're out shooting on location again?" Madison said, even though the feeling in her gut said they weren't. "Let's go check," she said, wishing she could do something to erase the shattered, disappointed look in Alyssa's eyes. She marched over to the door.

"Maddie ..."

"Come on," Madison said, yanking the door open. "Don't be scared. What's the worst that can happen? They throw us out again? Big deal."

25
too late

It was clear the moment they stepped through the door: They were too late. The hushed we-are-making-magic semi-dark interior was gone. Large overhead lights were on. A huge door on the side was open, blasting the place with sunlight. A big truck was backing up, emergency lights flashing and a steady beep-beeping warning the crew to get out of the way. There was activity, but it had a different quality to it. Sets were being dismantled, torn down. Two massive guys passed by carrying a bulky maroon sofa.

"Excuse me," Madison said. "We were wondering if *Plummet* is done or if you're just shooting somewhere else?"

"Done. Wrapped last night," said the beer-bellied man, plopping down his end of the sofa and wiping the sweat off his brow.

"Hey, Wade, stop slacking," the man on the other end growled.

"Dude," the beer-bellied man said, "have some manners. This young lady asked me a question, and it would be highly uncouth for me to ignore her." He hiked up his jeans, which was a good thing because his pants were precariously close to sliding off altogether.

"And Josh Lowe?" Even though she could feel Alyssa pinching the back of her arm, hard, Madison had to ask. "Is he wrapped too?"

"Sweetheart," the beer-bellied man said, hoisting up the sofa again, "he wrapped last Friday."

"Last Friday?" Madison echoed, feeling discombobulated.

"Yup, and you two young missies better hightail it out of here before you get in trouble."

"Come on," Alyssa hissed, grabbing Madison's arm and dragging her out.

Back outside, Alyssa charged down the road like a bulldozer. "He wrapped last Friday. Perfect. Great," Alyssa fumed. "So that means we wasted a precious five days of your vacation, and went behind my mother's back to tail my *stupid* father who isn't even *here*!"

"We didn't know," Madison said, half-jogging to keep up. "If we had known, we wouldn't have, but—"

"We could have gone to Disneyland! We could have used our stinky Super Soakers on that obnoxious Star Tours pest. We could have gone to the beach. I could have taught you how to surf. And it's all ruined now, because we only have three days left—"

"Four, I don't leave until—"

"You can't count Tuesday! You fly home on Tuesday. Tuesday doesn't count. We only have three days left and then you go home, and I'm stuck here in this stupid town, in this stupid life—"

"Your life's not stupid," Madison said, reaching out to pat her arm.

"Shut up!" Alyssa said, jerking away. "You don't know anything. Why did you try to make me see him?" she said, glaring at Madison angrily. "I was perfectly fine before you came along with your ..." Her face screwed up into a namby-pamby sneer. "Alyssa," she mimicked in a nasty high-pitched voice, "who's your father? Don't you want to know? Everyone wants to know who their father is."

"Alyssa, I ..."

"And now you've wasted our time, forcing me to chase after an . . ."—Alyssa's voice broke—"an illusion . . ." She was crying now, miserable, sad, lost. "Stuffing me full of fantasies . . ."—her shoulders bowed, her voice fading to a broken whisper—"that I could have a real father too . . . a dad like your dad and . . ."

Madison stepped forward, wrapping her arms tightly around her best friend. "I'm sorry," she said. "I am so sorry."

They stayed like that for a long time, until finally, Alyssa was able to stop crying, and then Madison was able to stop crying too.

26
bev

The girls were in the back seat of the car. Jessica was scrubbing her face with makeup-remover pads that she had snagged from the makeup trailer on their way to the car. "You are awful quiet back there," Jessica said, turning in her seat. "Are you all right?"

"Mm-hm . . ." Alyssa nodded. "Just tired is all."

"You would tell me if there was something wrong?" Jessica asked, her movement with the makeup pad on her face slowing. She looked so serious and sort of worried, but the effect was kind of funny too because the mascara was in the early stages of removal and had smeared into two dark raccoon circles around her eyes. "Was someone on the set rude to you?"

"No, Mom."

Jessica's eyes widened for a split second and then narrowed. "Inappropriate? Because if so, I swear to god—"

"Mom!" Alyssa said, cutting her off. "Everyone was fine. I'm just tired is all."

"Okay." Jessica nodded, her makeup pad resuming its circular motion. "But you know that if ever—" Jessica's cell phone rang. "Oh dang!" She rummaged in her purse, dug it out, and clicked it on. "Yes?" She listened for a second, her face lighting up. "Bev!" she exclaimed. "How are you? ... Uh-huh ..." She nodded. "Ooo, that sounds like a wonderful way to see my birthday in. I would love that. Let me check with the girls." Jessica cupped her hand around the phone. "Bev wants to know if we'd like to spend the weekend at her place."

"Yes," Alyssa said, perking up. "Absolutely. What a great idea!"

Jessica smiled and turned back to her conversation with her friend.

"You're going to love it!" Alyssa crowed. "That's the friend I was telling you about who has the beach house in Malibu. You're going to love her place. It is so cozy and homey. Kind of like a rich person's version of your family's house—no offence."

"None taken," Madison said, happy that Alyssa appeared to be snapping out of her melancholy.

"Mom," Alyssa said, tapping her mom on the shoulder, "when are we going to Bev's?"

"Hold on a second," Jessica said to her friend on the phone. She turned around. "What, honey?"

"When are we going?" Alyssa repeated.

"Well, whenever you like. Tonight? Tomorrow?"

"Let's go tonight," Alyssa said, her eyes sparkling.

"You aren't too tired?" Jessica asked.

"No, I feel great. How about you, Maddie?"

"I'm good," Madison replied.

"All right then," Jessica said. "Tonight it is." She turned back to the phone. "We're going to swing by the house, grab a few things, and be there"—she glanced at the clock on the dashboard—"in an hour to an hour and a half." She grinned over her shoulder at the girls and gave them a thumbs-up. "All right, Bev, see you soon!" she said and clicked the phone off.

"Whee!" Jessica said, tossing her makeup-removal pads up into the air. "Fun, fun, fun!"

27
the beach house

Jessica was behind the wheel as they soared down the Pacific Coast Highway in her powder-blue convertible with the top down. Madison had never ridden in a convertible before. It was a glorious feeling sitting in the back seat with Alyssa, the wind streaming through their hair, the tang and taste of the ocean air swirling around them. Nadine sat proudly in the front passenger seat, her ears flapping and her tongue hanging out, and a huge grin on her face.

The sun was setting over the ocean, sending streaks of orange, red, and gold across the sky. As it sank, the colours were at first more vivid, but when the ocean finally swallowed it up, the colours shifted. Lilac and a bruised purple added their streaks to the mix as the orange, red, and gold softened and gave way, until finally, there was just a trace, a remembrance of the sunset, and then that was gone too.

"So beautiful," Madison murmured.

"Yeah," Alyssa replied, still looking to the horizon as if fixing the image in her mind. "I'm going to paint it."

Madison smiled and felt proud by association. She wished she could paint one-tenth as well as her friend could, but she didn't say anything. She didn't want to interrupt her friend's creative process.

Once the sun set, the drop in temperature was instantaneous and darkness started to close around them. Madison shivered.

Jessica must have felt the chill too, because she pulled to the side of the road and pressed a button on the dashboard; the top of the convertible automatically unfolded itself from the storage compartment behind the back seat. It reminded Madison of a bird stretching out its wing.

Jessica punched in a CD, and as music filled the interior of the car, they were off again soaring down the highway. It must have been a track they listened to often because Jessica and Alyssa sang along. Madison didn't know the words but the melody was easy enough to follow, so she joined in with a "Hmm … la … la … hmm …"

The music rumbled around and through them. It felt like a smile that incorporated her whole being.

It was night when they arrived at Bev's house. And the second they walked through the front door, Madison could totally see why it reminded Alyssa of a rich person's version of Maddie's home. It was very cozy. There were baked brownies cooling, but still warm, on the counter, and Bev had a big pot of something that smelled savoury and delicious simmering on the stove. There were hugs and squeals when they arrived. Even Nadine got a special hug and scratch behind the ears.

The twin beds in the room the girls were sharing had homemade patchwork quilts of sunshine yellow, peach, and lilac. There was a pretty, multicoloured blown-glass bowl with an assortment of wrapped candies in it. "For us?" Madison asked.

Alyssa smiled and nodded. "I love it here," she said. And Madison could see why. It was beautiful and comfortable and welcoming.

They had their own bathroom and a door that led out to a deck that wrapped right around to the front of the house, where the ocean was. Madison could only see a tiny hint of the ocean by the pale light of the moon. But she could hear it, loud and clear: the rush of the waves crashing in, the water rushing forward, and then the sound of it receding, dragging sand particles in its wake. The air seemed much saltier than the ocean air in Oregon. She licked her lips and could taste the salt on them.

"We'll swim tomorrow," Alyssa said as they slid open the door from the deck to the living room and stepped inside, Nadine padding behind them like a comforting shadow.

Bev and Alyssa's mom were belly-laughing about something, sipping red wine out of long-stemmed glasses, and tucking into the warm brownies.

"My goodness," Alyssa said in a mock-adult voice. "Will you look at you two—brownies before dinner? Tsk-tsk …"

The grownups looked sheepish, but they laughed some more—they were having fun breaking the rules. It made Madison happy because it reminded her of a grownup version of Alyssa and herself.

28
chili dogs

By the time the girls woke up the next morning, the sun was already high in the sky. They had gone to bed late last night, stuffed to the gills. Dinner had been delicious chicken stewed in a savoury gravy, with tiny onions, bits of bacon, and little button mushrooms. Bev said it was a French dish called coq au vin. They had brownies for dessert and kept nibbling on them through the movie they watched in Bev's screening room.

And yes, there was popcorn. Alyssa had tucked the popcorn and truffle oil in a plastic bag and plopped it into her overnight bag. "Bev always likes to screen movies," she'd told Madison. And sure enough, after dinner it was movie time.

"I'll make the popcorn!" Alyssa announced.

Jessica and Bev were so surprised when Alyssa dashed to her room and returned to the kitchen with her ingredients in hand. She walked over to the stove and made the popcorn like a pro, and it was good. Alyssa's mom and Bev couldn't stop eating it. They said it was *the best* popcorn they had *ever* tasted!

Just remembering made Madison grin.

"Ready?" Alyssa asked. Madison glanced over at Alyssa, who was seated beside her on the bench at the Malibu Country Mart, her goopy chili dog poised in front of her mouth. Beyond Alyssa, a little boy in blue shorts was trying to shimmy up the leg of the large red hammerhead-man sculpture that was standing in the middle of the grassy section of the square.

"I'm ready," Madison replied, lifting her chili dog as well. It didn't look so special, just another greasy hot dog slathered in chili, but as it came closer to her mouth, she was already starting to understand the magic that was *this* chili dog. It smelled *sooo* good that she started involuntarily drooling.

"Set … aaand …" Alyssa said slowly, drawing out the anticipation. *"Bite!"*

Madison bit down and all the chili-cheddar-cheesy goodness filled her mouth. "Mmm," she said, shutting her eyes momentarily to taste it even better. "Yum!" She sighed happily.

"Delicious, huh?" Alyssa said, taking another big bite, chili overflowing and sliding down her fingers. Alyssa lapped up the escaping chili with her tongue before it got to her wrist. "And there is *no* way you can eat these babies neatly," she said with a grin, "so there is no point even trying."

Madison took another bite. "Mmm ..." she said again.

Alyssa laughed. "Okay, mission accomplished. If I can render the wordsmith of Ms. Elliot's fifth-grade class speechless, I've done my duty."

Madison swallowed. "Grade six now," she managed to get out. "We've graduated."

"Elementary students no more," Alyssa said, draping the back of her hand against her forehead like she was about to faint.

"Ooh, such a fine lady, Alyssa," Madison said, using her own fine-lady voice. "Of course, the smears of chili on your arm sort of mar the impression."

Alyssa glanced at her arm and laughed.

"Just a titch," Madison said, holding her own goopy forefinger and thumb around half an inch apart, her pinky quirked like she was drinking tea.

Both girls laughed. And then, they weren't laughing anymore. They were looking at each other, throats choked up.

"I can't believe we won't . . ." Alyssa said. Her voice trailed off, unable to finish.

"I know." Madison's eyes suddenly blurred with tears.

They stared down at their hot dogs, not hungry anymore.

All around them, life moved on. Children swung on the swing set, slid down the slide. Mothers passed by, pushing babies in designer strollers, tossing their sun-streaked hair.

"I'm going to miss you," Alyssa said, her voice rough.

"I'm going to miss you too." A fat tear dropped onto Madison's chili dog. And then another.

"Brrrrrr . . ." A girl in a yellow-striped shirt and jean shorts zoomed by, her arms outstretched like she was a plane.

Alyssa dug in the brown paper bag that the wrapped-up chili dogs had been in, pulled out some napkins, and handed a couple to Madison.

"Thanks," Madison said.

They both laid their chili dogs on the bench between them and wiped their faces, but it wasn't helping, because the next second they were wet again.

"What's wrong?" asked a little blond curly-haired boy. He looked about three and was lying on his belly in the warm sand looking up at them with big brown eyes. "Why are you sad?"

"Because," Alyssa explained—she was always so patient with little kids—"she's my best friend, but she lives in Oregon and I live here, and after this weekend ..." Alyssa could not go on.

"We aren't going to be able to see each other anymore," Madison said.

"But you are with each other now?" the little boy said.

"Yes." Alyssa nodded. "We are with each other now."

The boy tipped his head, genuinely curious. "So why be sad?"

"Good idea," Alyssa said, her voice gentle.

The boy went back to drawing patterns in the sand.

29
swimming in the ocean

Alyssa was right, Madison thought as she dove through another breaker. *The ocean is way warmer.* She glanced to her right, and there was Nadine with her nose up, making little snorting noises and dog-paddling beside her.

Nadine was really funny. She got nervous when she thought Alyssa or Madison were getting too far out. She would speed up her paddling to get in front of them and then nudge them with her head, herding them back toward the shore.

Madison thought it was hilarious, but Alyssa was not amused. "It's a pain," she complained. "It's not like we are even out that far. It's hard to bodysurf properly when your dumb dog won't let you swim more than a few yards out." But Alyssa was wrong. They could bodysurf fine, and truthfully, Madison was glad Nadine wouldn't let them go farther. Madison wasn't as strong a swimmer as Alyssa and wasn't crazy about going out so far that she wasn't able to stand up and feel her feet on the ground.

Madison looked over her shoulder out to sea. She could see a good swell coming. She treaded water, waiting for it, and when the swell almost reached her, she turned forward and started swimming the crawl as hard as she could, face down, eyes shut, her heart beating fast. Was she going to make it? Did she time it right? And then … *Yes!* She could feel the water swell beneath her. She launched her body into a gliding position with her arms straight in front, hands criss-crossed. A quick flutter kick with her legs to keep the momentum going as the powerful water picked up speed, and both Madison and the water surged forward faster and faster. Madison could feel the sand, grit, and water swirl around her as the ocean deposited her on the shore and then receded again. She lay back on the hard wet sand, exhilarated.

Madison sat up and turned back to the ocean. Flopping her wet, sand-encrusted hair out of her face, she spit particles of salty-sea grit out of her mouth. The sun was really bright, making her squint. She shaded her eyes and looked out.

Oh, Nadine, Madison thought, shaking her head. *You're going to get in trouble.* Alyssa, out farther than Nadine was comfortable with, was getting the full head-bump treatment.

"Nadine!" Alyssa yelled. "Stop it!" But Nadine wasn't listening. She'd just dodge Alyssa's shooing arms, dart in, and nudge her whenever there was an opening. "Sheesh. I'm trying to bodysurf here, and you made me miss that wave!"

"Hey, Nadine!" Madison called, slapping the ground enthusiastically beside her. "Here, girl. Come on! I've got a *treat*!" Not that she did, but she could always run to the house and get one.

Nadine ignored her.

"All right," Alyssa said, heading back to shore. "You've had your chance. I'm taking you back to Bev's house and tying you up."

Another dog, however, was not so deaf to Madison's cajoling. The next thing she knew, a wiggling, licking, soaking wet bundle of fur launched itself into her lap.

"Aaah!" Madison shrieked. But she shrieked because she was startled, not because she was scared. *That's weird,* she thought. *I guess I must not be scared of dogs anymore.* Madison wrapped her arms around the wiggling grey-and-beige German Shepherd puppy with black-and-white patches and gave it a hug. She got an *arf!* in response. It looked kind of familiar. The puppy slurped at her face. *Or maybe,* Madison thought, running her forefinger in the groove between the puppy's eyes, *it's this dog I'm not scared of, and Nadine, of course.* The puppy gazed at Madison with an adoring look and then rolled onto his back, gangly legs waving in the air, showing off his tender, pink baby tummy. His expression said, "belly rub, please?" So she did.

Alyssa was wading out of the ocean with her hand firmly latched on to Nadine's collar. Nadine didn't seem to realize she was in trouble. The dog appeared quite pleased with herself and had the biggest mission-accomplished dog grin on her satisfied face. Madison laughed. *Silly old dog.*

"Gus!" someone called. "Get off her lap, you muddy mutt."

Gus? Madison thought. *The name sounded familiar too.* She looked up from the cuddly puppy. A tall tanned man wearing grey swimming trunks and running shoes was jogging toward her.

"I am so sorry," he said. "My pup hasn't learned manners yet."

The man had a beautiful smile and blond hair and looked a lot like …

"Gus, you are such a mischievous scamp."

Josh Lowe? Huh? Madison blinked. *Nope, he is still there and it's still him.*

"He didn't hurt you, did he?" Josh Lowe, Alyssa's dad-but-not-her-dad, was looking right at her. Talking *to* her.

Madison shook her head. *Speak ... mouth.* "No," she managed to squeak. "He's just a puppy. ALYSSA!" *Oh dear. Did she just yell that?*

"Whaa?!" Josh Lowe leapt back startled, and the puppy in Madison's lap flipped onto his feet. Madison snagged his collar. Her brain was working in overdrive even if her mouth wasn't. *Keep the puppy until Alyssa gets here. That way her father-who's-not-a-father can't go jogging off into the sunset before Alyssa gets a chance to talk with him face to face.* Of course, the minute she grabbed his collar, the puppy no longer wanted to be in her lap. He started twisting and turning and trying to wiggle out of her grasp. Madison didn't let go. The puppy started to yip.

"My friend—" Madison explained, talking over the racket the puppy was making, "she loves puppies. ALYSSA!" Madison was starting to sweat. If Alyssa didn't arrive soon, Josh Lowe might start wondering why Madison was hanging on to his dog.

"What?" Alyssa said, marching up with Nadine in tow. She had a scowl on her face. Madison ignored it.

"Look at this adorable puppy! His name's

Gus, right?" Madison said, turning to Josh Lowe. "Such a cute name."

Josh Lowe turned.

Alyssa froze, her hand releasing Nadine, who strolled over and smelled the puppy's bottom then nudged him with her nose. Gus flipped over on his back again, his tongue lolling out the side of his mouth. Nadine flopped down with a grunt on the sand beside Madison and closed her eyes, basking in the warmth of the sun. Gus pounced on Nadine. She ignored him.

Gus ... Madison thought. *Cute German Shepherd puppy ... soft fur ... Aha!* Madison grinned. *Mystery solved. He's the puppy from the studio.*

"That's quite a beaut you have there," Josh said, glancing admiringly at Nadine. "I was thinking of getting a Rotti, but then I fell in love with this little guy."

Alyssa didn't say anything. Her mouth was hanging open. *Must still be in shock,* Madison thought. *Well, it's up to me then to keep up the conversation until she finds her tongue.* "I can see why," Madison said. "He is adorable."

Gus was now straddling Nadine's back and attempting to fit her whole ear in his mouth. She tolerated it for a little bit and then shook her head and shoulders, and he went flying off her back. Gus rolled, his legs going every which way.

"Have we met?" Madison heard Josh say to Alyssa. Madison wanted to turn and watch, but she kept her gaze on the dogs. Gus was back on his feet and bounding over to Nadine again.

"No," Alyssa said.

"Are you sure?" Josh asked. "You look so familiar."

Madison wasn't looking, but she was listening, all right, and she was waiting for Alyssa's answer.

Alyssa was silent.

Okay, enough is enough. Madison turned, and it was a good thing too, because Alyssa wasn't even looking at her dad. She was twisting her hands and staring toward the dogs, but her eyes looked blank, so she obviously wasn't looking at the dogs, and her cheeks were flaming red. It was clear that Alyssa wasn't going to be speaking any time soon. *Well, that's what friends are for,* Madison thought.

"Maybe she looks familiar because her mom is Jessica Ashton."

Alyssa's head snapped up. She gave Madison a dagger stare, but Madison didn't let it stop her. "Jessica Ashton, the actress. Do you know her?"

Josh didn't answer, just looked at her like he was trying to make sense of the words.

"Because," Madison continued blithely, "maybe you see a family resemblance?" Madison heard Alyssa gasp, but she didn't look at her because if she did, she would probably lose her nerve.

"Jessica Ashton?" Josh looked back at Alyssa. "Huh. You don't say."

"Do you know her?" Madison asked.

"I was in love with her," he said, still looking at Alyssa, a warm smile breaking across his face. "It was many, many years ago. But I still think of her often."

Alyssa was looking at him now, her eyes dark and vulnerable and full of questions.

"Such a beautiful woman, inside and out," he said, lost in memories. "She was the one who got away."

"Hey," Madison said, leaping to her feet. "I have an idea! It's Jessica's birthday tomorrow, and we're throwing a little surprise party." Alyssa's face swivelled from his face to hers. *Is that shock, horror, or scared delight on Allie's face?* Madison wondered. *Oh well, in too deep now.* "A very last-minute little surprise birthday party, but you would be more than welcome to come!"

"Really? You think it would be all right?"

"Of course!" Madison said jovially, her voice way too loud. She could feel her face heating up. "The more the merrier! It's a birthday party after all."

He blinked. He had a slightly stunned look on his face, as if he was a Martian trying to pretend he understood the language. He looked at Alyssa again and shook his head as if to clear it. "I can't get over the resemblance," he said.

"Yes, Alyssa has her mom's unusual eyes," Madison said, watching him closely. "Her hair colour is different though …"

"Maddie," Alyssa hissed.

Okay, she had gone too far with the hints. "We are staying at Bev's house for this weekend." Madison turned around and pointed at it. "It's the bluish-green-grey one with the white trim right there. Can you see it? It's three houses over. The party starts at …" *When do grownup parties start?* Madison thought, suddenly panicked. *Um … late. Later than kid parties. Dang! My parents didn't really do the whole party thing, and if I say the wrong time, he'll know I'm making it up.*

"Seven-thirty," Alyssa piped up.

"That's right," Madison said, relief rushing through her. "The party starts at seven-thirty p.m. Hope to see you there."

"It's a tempting offer. I'll give it some thought," he said. "Come on, Gus, time to go." He snapped his fingers and, surprisingly, Gus came. "It was a pleasure chatting with you."

"You too," Madison said.

"Glad to have met you," Alyssa said, but she spoke so quietly Madison was pretty sure he didn't hear.

They watched him jog down the beach. "Seven-thirty tomorrow night!" Madison called. "Be there or be square!"

He turned and waved, jogging backwards, a grin on his face, Gus frolicking at his heels.

"Be there or be square?" Alyssa said, shaking her head. "Where did you get that one?"

"Okay, maybe that wasn't the best parting phrase—"

"I'll say," Alyssa said, a reluctant smile blooming on her face.

"But we've got bigger problems on our plate." The two girls looked at each other, the magnitude of what Madison promised landing with a thud. "Like how to get a party together by tomorrow night." Madison chewed her thumbnail nervously.

"Don't stress yourself out," Alyssa said, shaking her head. "He's not going to show."

"But on the off chance he does," Madison said, "we can't have him show up to just the four of us eating some dinner and watching a chick flick on TV."

Alyssa's eyes widened. "Uh-oh. How are we going to pull this off?" She started pacing in small worried circles. "Okay. First of all, we have to make sure it's all right with Bev. Next, we won't tell my mom about the party, but I have to give her the heads-up that we bumped into him today and there is a slight possibility that he might drop by sometime and say hello. I don't think he will, but just in case, I don't want her to be blindsided."

Madison nodded, a nervous knot forming in her stomach. "Yeah, you're right. It wouldn't be fair. And you can tell her," Madison said, swallowing hard, "that it's my fault. I'm the one who invited him."

"I didn't stop you," Alyssa said. "We are in this together." She stopped her pacing and attempted to smile. "Don't look so worried. It's already done. And there's no undoing it even if we wanted to." She rolled her shoulders, unfolded her arms, and shook them out like a boxer stepping into the ring. "Okay, the party. We can't pull it off without Bev. She could help us with food and decorations, and can call some of Mom's friends . . ."

Madison was the one pacing now, wringing her hands. "But what if your mom hits the roof and doesn't want to stay here anymore, decides to return to your house in L.A.? What if Bev says no?" Alyssa's and Madison's eyes locked.

"Then," Alyssa said, "we are well and truly screwed." And that pronouncement was enough to send the two girls sprinting toward Bev's beach house, a mix of excitement and nerves thrumming through them.

30
the party

"Would you care for a chili-glazed chicken skewer?" one of the white-clad catering staff asked.

"No, thank you," Madison said, even though they looked delicious. *This must be costing Bev an awful lot of money.* Madison glanced around guiltily. *Can she afford it? Me and my stupid ideas. I just thought we'd make chips and dip and put out a bowl of cashews. I didn't realize this was the way they do parties in California. Oh dear, oh dear. I never should have suggested this.* Madison sighed. At least Alyssa's mom hadn't gotten mad when they told her about bumping into Josh Lowe and that he said he might drop by. "Oh, honey," Jessica had said, pulling a worried Alyssa in for a hug. "He's a very busy man. Best not to get your hopes up, okay?"

The party was in full swing. At least a hundred people had shown up. One hundred people! Who knew one hundred people well enough to invite them to a party Saturday afternoon and have them show up, impromptu, on Sunday?

Apparently, Bev did. When the girls arrived back at the house from the beach, Alyssa had stuck her head in the kitchen. "Hey, Bev," she'd called. "Something's wrong with the outdoor shower. We can't turn it on."

Bev handed the box of tea to Jessica. "You're on tea duty. I'll be right back."

The minute the kitchen door was closed safely behind her, Alyssa and Madison had whispered, "Shhhhh ..." as they pulled her around to the back of the house. They told her their idea, and Bev was instantly on board. "What a wonderful idea!" she exclaimed. "Why didn't I think of that?"

"I make pretty good onion chip dip," Madison had said. "People always like chips and dip to nibble on."

"And we make killer chocolate-chip cookies," Alyssa said.

"And popcorn," Madison said.

"And popcorn," Alyssa said, flashing a smile at her friend. "And we could buy some root beer and ice cream and make root beer floats and ..."

She turned to look at Madison. "Maddie, have you ever made a cake?"

"Sure," Madison said. "We could make the cake."

"So, Bev, you wouldn't need to worry," Alyssa said. "We'd do all the preparation and cleanup. But what we don't have is a list of Mom's friends or their phone numbers. We were hoping that maybe you could invite them and tell them how to get here?"

"No problem," Bev said. "Watch this." She picked up her cell phone off the table. "Hello, Rex. I'm going to throw a little birthday shindig for Jessica tomorrow. It's a surprise, so hush-hush. Now, I'll need you to call a few people for me and ..."

And that was it. Bev had snuck out of the room every now and then to answer the phone calls that were flying back and forth, and by suppertime, the whole thing was organized: Guests were coming; Bev's favourite caterer had been cajoled into squeezing her in; and a bartender and a DJ had been hired. Bev in action was a miracle to behold.

The hard part had been figuring a way to get Jessica out of the house so they could set up, but even that was not a problem for Bev. She had booked a spa day for Jessica. "You can't say no!"

Bev insisted as she and the girls dropped Jessica off. "It's a birthday gift, love. A day of relaxation." Bev leaned across Jessica and pushed open her car door.

"But—" Jessica stammered, looking confused. "I thought we were going to—"

"A change of plans," Bev had said breezily, giving Jessica a little shove. "Out you get. And not to worry, a spa lunch is included. Enjoy!" she said, shutting the car door behind Jessica, revving the engine, and wiggling her fingers jauntily out her window. "We'll pick you up in five hours. Ta-ta!" And Bev, Alyssa, and Madison had zoomed off, cackling at their cleverness.

But now, for Madison, standing on Bev's porch, looking at all the fancy people drinking wine and nibbling on the super-fancy food that was being walked around the room on silver platters by white-clad waiters, it was not a fun evening. First off, she felt guilty about the cost. Second, there was the guilt about Alyssa.

Alyssa was good at this party stuff. Madison never would have believed it, given how shy she was at school, but in this setting, she shone. Her mom was keeping Alyssa close by her side and included in the conversations, chatting to the people that Alyssa already knew and introducing her to the ones she didn't. Alyssa would smile up at them and talk with them like they were equals, her blond hair shining like spun gold in the glow of the white fairy lights that the girls had strung that afternoon over the potted plants, banisters, and the tree by the front door. Alyssa looked like an enchanted princess in a fairy tale—complete with the beauty, the smile, the famous movie-star mother, and the slight bruised, hurt quality behind the eyes that apparently only Madison could see.

He hadn't come.

They had done all this work to pull off a last-minute party, and for what?

Not to mention, Alyssa's broken heart. She was acting all brave and being the perfect daughter, without a worry in the world, standing gracefully at Jessica's side. But Madison knew she was hurting. This morning Madison had watched her friend go through and discard every outfit she'd packed. She was right beside her when Alyssa worked up the courage to ask Bev if she could borrow some money to go shopping, which was as out of character for her as Jughead from the Archie comics voluntarily kissing a girl. It had taken Alyssa a long time to find just the right dress.

After the lights were strung and everything was set, the girls got dressed. Madison noticed that when Alyssa was buttoning her dress, her hands were shaking.

Stupid Josh Lowe! Madison wanted to punch something. After all of that careful preparation and Alyssa's cautious, hopeful caring, the jerk hadn't even bothered to come.

Madison was mad at him, but she was mad at herself even more. Why had she poked her nose into something that wasn't her business? What kind of friend was she? A bad one! Talking her friend into spending a good portion of their vacation stalking her dad-but-not-her-dad at the studio. Inviting him to a pretend party. Forcing her mother's friend to throw one. Getting Alyssa's hopes up that maybe dreams do come true.

Madison shook her head bitterly. *With a friend like me, who needs an enemy? It's probably a good thing Alyssa's moved back to L.A. She's probably better off without me.* Madison's eyes filled with tears. She turned her back to the party, so no one could see, and faced the ocean with her eyes shut. The wood of the deck rail was still holding a little bit of warmth from the day's sun. She forced herself to think about other things ... the feel of the wood, the wind on her face. She focused on the song playing softly in the background, of love lost and love found.

She listened to the sound of the surf going in and out. And the tears lightened and she was glad, because she was not going to ruin Alyssa's mom's party by being the weird girl crying in the corner. Humming slightly, like she was perfectly content and daydreaming, she edged her way to the side deck, keeping her head facing out like she was enjoying the view. When she reached the unlit shadowed part along the side of the house, she walked briskly to their bedroom, slid the door open, and stepped inside.

It was a relief to be away from all those people. For a moment, Madison was tempted to get into her pyjamas and crawl into bed, but she didn't. She went into the bathroom, washed her face in cold water, patted it dry, ran a brush through her hair, took a deep breath, and stepped back out through the sliding door to the side deck.

She stood there for a second, in the comfort of the shadows, watching the party from the darkness.

And that's when she saw him.

Josh Lowe, coming up the steps from the beach! Madison's heart leapt with happiness for her friend. She dashed to the top of the stairs. "You came!" she said.

He smiled. "Yeah," he said. "Sorry I'm late. I forgot I had a dinner meeting with a producer that I couldn't get out of. Does Jessica know you invited me?"

"Well," Madison said, "it was a surprise birthday party, so she didn't know anyone was coming, but don't worry, we mentioned we met you on the beach. She'll be happy you're here, and I know Alyssa will be." Madison could feel his hesitation, so she ran down the stairs and grabbed his arm before he could change his mind and go back home. It was funny. Who would have thought a fancy movie star like Josh Lowe would ever be shy.

Madison tugged him forward. "By the way," she said, "Jessica isn't married or in love with anyone right now. Not that it's any of my business, but just in case you were wondering, I thought I'd let you know."

He laughed. "You are a funny kid," he said, looking at her in an affectionate manner. *He would make Alyssa a really nice father!* Madison thought.

"What are you grinning about?" he asked.

"Oh, nothing," Madison said. "I'm just happy you came. Come on. Let's go find them." When they arrived at the top of the stairs, it was just the two of them for a moment, but then one person glanced over and saw that it was Josh Lowe, did a double take, and whispered something to the woman next to her, who craned her head to take a discreet peek. It was like a rippling-wave effect; within seconds, a good portion of the people on the deck either saw him or heard the whispered rumour that Josh Lowe was in attendance.

"The birthday girl is over there," Madison said. "I'll take you to say hello."

They wove their way through the crowd. It took a little while because everyone they passed wanted to say hello, shake hands, tell him how much they liked his work, or talk about a project they had that he would be perfect in. But with Madison's help, they kept moving forward. And then suddenly, it was like a pathway opened up, and at the other end of it was Alyssa with her mom, standing together and looking so beautiful it made Madison's throat ache. Alyssa said something and her mom laughed, and Alyssa laughed too, and then, as if they felt him, they both looked up. And there he was: Josh Lowe walking toward them, holding out a small brightly wrapped present that had an orange bow with cheerful pink-and-yellow dots.

Alyssa's face lit up, like Christmas had come early.

Jessica looked startled for a second, and then the look was gone. "Josh," she said in that low, husky voice she had—totally composed, except for the telltale flush on her cheeks. "Such a pleasure to see you," she drawled.

"Hi, Jessica," Josh said. And Madison could tell by the way he was looking at her that he was still in love with her. "It's been way too long," he said, his voice so quiet that Madison almost didn't hear. "I've missed you," he said. Just like that. Heartfelt. Simple. Straightforward. True.

Alyssa grabbed Madison's hand and squeezed. Madison squeezed back. Happy. So happy.

"Oh, Josh," Jessica said with a reluctant smile. "What am I going to do with you?"

Josh grinned. He handed her the gift. "Happy Birthday, Jessica."

Later that night, most everyone had left. The caterer had packed up; the DJ and bartender had gone. A few guests lingered—talking, sipping wine. Someone had gotten out a guitar and was strumming it softly.

The girls were tucked in bed, tired but unable to sleep. "Maybe they are going to get together again. What do you think?" Alyssa said, flipping onto her side to face Madison.

If it had been before tonight and before Madison's revelations and vow to herself to be a better friend, she would have spun this fairy tale out to a happy-ever-after conclusion. But this was reality, and it was Alyssa's heart and Alyssa's life. "I don't know," Madison said.

They were quiet for awhile, listening to the lingering remnants of the party, to the ocean rushing in and out.

"I really like him," Alyssa said.

"Me too." Madison yawned. She was tired, but she didn't want to sleep, because when she woke up, it would be Monday and after Monday was Tuesday and that was the day she was going home.

"Do you think he's still here?" Alyssa asked.

"I don't know." Madison yawned again. The sleep waves were starting to win.

"Let's go see," Alyssa said.

And even though Madison was tired, she wasn't about to say no. Alyssa's can't-sleep excitement reminded Madison of her little sister, Gina, on Christmas Eve. Gina always wanted Madison to sneak into the living room with her, after their parents were asleep, to make a wish on the Christmas tree.

"Good idea," Madison said, stifling another yawn.

The girls got out of bed, quietly and carefully slid the sliding glass door open, and stepped outside, Alyssa leading the way. They stuck to the shadows along the side of the house as they made their way toward the remaining party-goers. Madison could see that on the right side of the deck almost everyone was gone. There was a group of four guys sitting around the table arguing politics. A really pretty dark-haired woman sat on one of the guy's laps.

Alyssa cautiously poked her head around the corner of the house and then pulled it back quickly. "He's still here," she whispered, her eyes glowing. "Take a peek." She switched positions with Madison.

Madison looked around the corner, and there were Josh and Alyssa's mom, sitting in the far corner of the deck by themselves on lounge chairs that had been shoved together. They were sitting in separate chairs that were reclined halfway back. Their bodies were facing each other. Madison couldn't see Josh's face, but she could see Alyssa's mom's. She was saying something, and then his hand gently smoothed a strand of hair to the side of her face and he took her hand. She stopped talking and just looked at him, her head tipped slightly to the side. Madison could tell they liked each other.

"What's going on?" Alyssa whispered.

"Here," Madison whispered, "let's trade again." And so they did.

"Oh my goodness," Alyssa whispered. "He just kissed her hand!" Alyssa swung around to face Madison. "He just kissed her hand, and she didn't pull away!"

"Hmm ..." Madison said. "Maybe we better go back to bed?"

"Yeah." Alyssa nodded. "This is private."

The girls scampered along the side of the house, through the door, and hopped into bed. They pulled the covers up, shivering slightly from the cool night.

"I was thinking," Madison said as she snuggled down into bed. "Maybe your mom would let you come spend Thanksgiving Break with us. My dad makes the best turkey stuffing you ever tasted, and we could make the pies and—"

"Oh, Maddie," Alyssa said, "that would be so much fun! And then we wouldn't have to be so sad, because it wouldn't be 'goodbye'—it would be 'see you later.'"

"That's what I was thinking," Madison said, hopeful happiness bubbling in her chest.

"Or maybe ..." Alyssa said, sitting upright, her eyes sparkling, "Mom would let me come sooner? Like next month for the last couple weeks in August, to boost our spirits before we head off to the scary wilds of junior high!"

"Do you think she would let you?"

"Yeah!" Alyssa beamed at her friend, the moonlight streaming through the window lighting up her face. "I bet she will. I just have to approach it right."

"We have a plan," Madison said in a deep radio-announcer voice, which caused both girls to chuckle. Madison sighed happily.

Best friends.

The guitarist wasn't playing anymore. Maybe he went home, or started talking to someone, or went for a walk. The only music now was the push and pull of the ocean ... in and out ... in and out ...

"This has been ..." Alyssa said just before she drifted off to sleep, "the best day I ever had." Madison smiled, a peaceful happiness filling her, and a moment later she was asleep as well.

31
early morning

It was still dark when Alyssa's mom gently nudged Madison and Alyssa awake. "Sorry, girls," she whispered, as if talking softly would make the awakening easier, "but they've switched the order of scenes, and I'm up first." She clicked on the bedside light.

Alyssa groaned and flung her arm over her eyes. "What time is it?" she mumbled.

"Four-twenty," Alyssa's mom said. "It's an unfortunate switch, but that's the reality of set life. I'll need you packed and ready to go in fifteen ..."—Jessica glanced at the clock—"actually fourteen minutes. I'll drop you girls and Nadine off at home and then head on to the studio."

The girls stumbled out of bed. Somehow, fifteen minutes later they were in the convertible and zooming down the Pacific Coast Highway, Alyssa and her mom in the front and Madison and Nadine snuggled in the back.

Alyssa's mom looked happy. She couldn't have gotten much sleep, but one would never know it looking at her. She was glowing, a slight smile on her face as she drove. The highway was pretty empty—only an occasional car every few miles, the passing headlights briefly lighting up the interior of their car before sending them back into the quiet of the dark.

Madison leaned her cheek against the cool glass of the window. It was kind of peaceful being up so early, the rest of the world asleep.

"Did you tell him?" Alyssa asked, looking over at her mom. No one needed to ask what she was talking about. They all knew.

"No." Jessica shook her head. "I didn't."

"Are you going to?"

"I don't know," Jessica said. "We'll wait and see." She glanced over at her daughter. "Why, do you think I should?"

Madison saw a myriad of emotions and thoughts flicker across her friend's face. "I don't know," Alyssa finally said, her words coming slowly as if she was still figuring out how she felt. "I think you're right to wait and see. We are pretty happy how we are ... so we don't want to mess that up. He seems nice, but I think we should get to know him better—make sure this would be a happy thing for all of us before making that leap."

"Hmm. That makes sense," Alyssa's mom said.

The sky was starting to lighten. The pitch-black had shifted to charcoal grey. Madison tilted her head and looked up. There were fewer stars visible in the sky, and the slice of moon was saying goodbye as well.

"How did you get to be so wise?" Alyssa's mom said, her voice warm and affectionate with a touch of pride, as she placed her hand over her daughter's.

"Oh," Alyssa said, smiling back at her, "I guess I inherited it from you."

32
payback time

The plan for Monday had been to make the long-awaited trip to Disneyland. But when Jessica dropped the girls off, they were still pretty tired from the big events of the night before, so instead of eating breakfast and getting ready to go, they went back to bed.

When they awoke it was almost ten.

"Oh dear," Alyssa said, grimacing at the bedside clock. "We slept in. By the time we get to Disneyland, the crowds are going to be ginormous!" She sighed. "Oh well," she said, heaving herself to an upright position. "If we want to get on any rides at all, we'd better get going."

"You know what?" Madison said, rubbing the sleep from her eyes. "I'm fine to stay home."

"Really?" Alyssa said, looking at her hopefully. "You wouldn't be disappointed?"

"No," Madison replied. "I wouldn't be disappointed at all. I think I would be relieved."

"Are you just saying that," Alyssa said, "because you know I'm not a big Disneyland freak? Because I'm happy to go. Seriously, I wouldn't go for many people, but I would do it for you. And you've never been—"

"No. Actually, I'd rather stay here and have a peaceful last day with you, puttering around the house, swimming, maybe making some cookies. Because, truthfully, the idea of spending a couple hours in the car getting there and back, racing around battling the crowds, standing in long lines in the pounding heat seems kind of like ..."—Madison paused, trying to find the right words—"I don't know ... It would feel kind of frenetic."

"Frenetic?" Alyssa said.

"Frenetic. Like racing around trying to grasp at a good time instead of just kicking back and enjoying each other's company."

"Well, if you're sure?" Alyssa said.

"I'm sure," Madison replied. "Besides, who knows what adventures we'll get into around here?"

"Yeah, right," Alyssa scoffed. "In this boring neighbourhood?"

◇

Madison leaned out a little bit farther, one hand holding on to the stepladder, the other reaching as far as she could. She felt the large grapefruit-sized lemon bump against her fingertips.

"Almost . . ." Alyssa called from below where she was steadying the ladder. "You're almost there. Good job."

Madison nodded. She couldn't reply because she had the bottom edge of her T-shirt tucked tight between her teeth to create a carrying pouch for her load of fresh-picked, beautiful, juicy lemons. She could feel the wet splotch on the fabric gripped in her teeth growing bigger—no matter how hard she tried to control her saliva, the tart-sweet fragrance of the sun-warmed lemons was making her drool.

She stretched out a touch further and was able to get her fingers a third of the way around the huge lemon, but when she tried to get a grip, it bobbed out of her hand.

"Be careful," Alyssa said, looking up at her anxiously. "Don't fall."

"Mmggffsss," Madison said, stretching a bit more. It was hot. She could feel a trickle of sweat running down the side of her face. Her jaw was getting a little tired from the weight of the shirt-full of lemons.

"Why don't you come down. We have enough lemons," Alyssa said.

But Madison was determined. This lemon was the biggest—the beaut—and she was determined to—

"HEY!" A loud voice blasted the quiet of the Ashton estate.

"Aaaahh!" Madison yelped. Startled, she accidentally let go of the ladder. Lemons spilled from her shirt, everything suddenly seeming to switch into slow motion.

She saw herself falling, reminded herself to tuck her head to her chest to protect it. She saw the lemons—orbs of translucent yellow-tinged beauties with traces of green—tumbling with her, saw the dappled light of sun through the leaves of the trees … She could hear Alyssa crying out, could hear the dodo-brain on the bullhorn bellowing, "JESSICA, BABY! YOU HOME?" … And then she landed—bounced once, twice, pounding the air out of her lungs. She could taste dust and blood … must have bitten her tongue.

Alyssa's worried face popped into view. "Maddie! Oh my god! Are you okay?"

Madison nodded, her head was ringing. "I got it," she said, cradling the enormous lemon that was the size of a baby's head to her chest.

"You scared me to death," Alyssa said. "Are you sure you're all right?"

Madison tentatively wiggled her arms and legs. "Phew," she said with a relieved smile. "Everything works."

"MISS ASHTON!" the guy on the bullhorn brayed. "COME ON OUT! DON'T BE SHY. I GOT SOME FOLKS HERE THAT WANT TO MEET YOU."

"And now," Madison said, getting to her feet and dusting off her hands. "It's *payback* time!" She liked the way she said it, like an old cowboy in a Western. And she could tell Alyssa liked it too, because Alyssa got this focused, I-eat-rattlesnakes-raw grin on her face that made Madison laugh out loud.

"Let's go!" Alyssa bellowed, her fist thrusting into the air as she led the charge down the slope, through the lemon trees, across the backyard, and into the garage where they grabbed their stinky Super Soaker weapons out of the fridge. "Ahhh! Nice and cold," Alyssa cackled.

The two girls sprinted out of the garage, around the side of the house, and over to the large knobby tree whose thick branches hung over the seven-foot-high grey wall that surrounded the exterior of the property.

Alyssa handed her Super Soaker to Madison, as per their plan, kicked off her sneakers, and shimmied up the tree. "Okay, your turn."

Madison passed the two Super Soakers up to Alyssa, kicked off her flip-flops, and shimmied up the tree. She scraped some skin off her left knee, but it was no big deal.

"YOOO-HOOO! WE ARE WAITING, JESSICA! WHY ARE YOU PRETENDING TO BE SOOOO SHY?"

Alyssa peered through the branches. "We need to get a bit higher," she said, handing the water guns back to Madison. As Madison watched Alyssa climb higher, she felt a wave of sadness—she was going to miss hanging out with her. "Hey, daydreamer," Alyssa called, one arm slung around a thick branch, the other reaching down with a saucy snap of her fingers, "time's a-wasting."

Madison handed off the water guns and scrambled up the remaining distance until she was perched beside her friend. It was a good spot. Madison could see the obnoxious guy with the bullhorn, the crowd of tourists, and the open-top blue shuttle bus with Star Tours!

emblazoned on the side, along with a multitude of large yellow stars. She could see them, but they couldn't see her. Madison and Alyssa were totally hidden among the large green boughs of the tree.

"JESSIE-BAYBEH! WE AREN'T LEAVING," the guy bleated into the bullhorn, twirling the keys to the shuttle bus on his forefinger. He still hadn't washed his hair—greasy strands hung out from under the stupid moth-eaten straw cowboy hat he had perched on his head.

"Okay," Alyssa said, cocking her gun. "Are you ready?"

"Affirmative." Madison nodded, cocking her gun as well and raising it up to her shoulder.

"SO GET OFF YOUR HIGH HORSE. COME ON OUTSIDE AND TAKE A FEW PICTURES WITH MY COMPADRES. *COMPRENDE?*"

"I'll compadres you," Alyssa said with a grim Clint Eastwood smile. "It's party time."

Both girls let fly with the stinky water, both barrels blazing. Madison had caught a whiff of the stink before—a small amount had leaked during the scramble up the tree—but it was nothing like the stench that was released when the liquid shot out of the tips of their guns. Great powerful arcs of water shot into the air and headed for their target. Madison wasn't sure whose stink stream went where. All she knew for sure was that *splat*, one of them got the big-mouthed jerk right in the chest.

"WHHAAAA!" he squawked, his eyes growing to the size of saucers, his head tipping up to gawk at the sky. "What the—" he sputtered, and *sploosh*, the second stink stream landed right in his mouth! It was hilarious. He started hopping around like Rumpelstiltskin, spitting like a madman, dropping his bullhorn, and yanking on his tongue with his hand to try to get the taste off.

"Ahem ..." Alyssa said in a fine-lady voice, her pinky extended. "I guess the taste leaves a little to be desired"—which made Madison laugh even harder.

"Shall we?" Madison said, trying to put on a fine-lady voice as well.

"Madison," Alyssa said, arching a fine lady's disapproving eyebrow, "how many times must I tell you? Fine ladies do *not* snort through their nose when they laugh. They go, 'tee-hee-hee.'"

Which, of course, made both of them laugh even more. They cocked their Super Soakers and let them rip again. Unfortunately, their aim wasn't as good since they were half doubled over with laughter. Their shots went awry, and the next thing they knew, the Crawfish Smelly Jelly Sticky Liquid concoction had sprayed across the crowd of camera-toting, celebrity-gawking Star Tours tourists.

Shrieks and then howls erupted as they flew for the safety of the shuttle bus. It was hilarious! It was heaven! The girls managed to get a few more pumps in as the bozo-brain crawled after his precious bullhorn that had rolled into the bushes. One of Madison's shots got him right on the butt. They drenched him some more as he raced to the shuttle bus yowling like a wet cat. And got another shot off as he leapt inside and was yanking the door shut. Gears grinding, tires burning rubber, the shuttle bus squealed out of the driveway and took off like the devil himself was chasing it.

Madison and Alyssa stayed up in that tree for awhile—even though they smelled pretty bad. They stayed up there, legs dangling, cheeks and tummies sore from laughing so much. They stayed there, reliving the greasy-haired guy's glorious defeat. They stayed there, best friends forever, with a glow in their hearts and the biggest grins ever on their faces.

"That," Alyssa said, finally breaking the happy silence, "was extremely satisfying."

33
in between

"We are starting our descent to the Eugene airport," a voice over the airplane loudspeaker said. "Please make sure that your seat belts are securely fastened and that your seats and tray tables are in an upright and locked position."

Madison checked her seat belt. It was secure. Her chair was already in the upright position, her tray table too, so there was nothing left to do but wait. She sighed and gazed out the window at the patches of land, dotted with the occasional house. It was weird to think that in each one of those houses there was a family living out their lives. People she would never know, and never meet, who didn't know a Madison Stokes existed, and didn't care that two hours ago she had said goodbye to the best friend she'd ever had.

Madison leaned her head back against the headrest and squeezed her eyes shut, trying to contain her feelings. She didn't know why she was feeling so emotional. Alyssa was already plotting how to convince her mom to let her visit Madison next month. Which would be *so* much fun. It was silly to be sad. Besides, Madison's family sacrificed to give her this vacation, and she was determined not to get off the plane and greet them with red-rimmed eyes.

She thought about her trip, about hanging out on the studio lot and seeing behind the scenes of how TV shows were shot. She thought about last night and how Jessica had taken them to that fancy restaurant for dinner. Inside the restaurant, they sat in a section that was open to the night sky. There was a big fireplace with a real wood fire roaring inside, and when the food arrived at their table, it looked like beautiful art on a plate—and it tasted *so* good. She thought about later, lying in bed, and how she and Alyssa couldn't sleep, so they put on their swimsuits and snuck outside, towels tucked under their arms. Nadine padded along beside them across the damp lawn, through the dark to the pool. They slipped silently into the water and swam, Nadine keeping watch, night-blooming jasmine scenting the air, and a million stars twinkling overhead. Special. It was a special, magical, perfect last night.

And as Madison sat there, while the airplane slowly descended, bringing her closer and closer to home, she thought about Josh Lowe and the way he and Alyssa's mom looked at each other. Madison could tell there were feelings, and thinking about it gave her happy shivers. *Wouldn't it be cool if they fell in love all over again and got married and*—Madison stopped herself mid-thought. *No,* she admonished herself. *Stop doing that. What will be, will be.* But even so, she was glad Alyssa promised to keep her updated.

The wheels of the plane thumped against the tarmac, brakes squealed, and jet propellers roared as they reversed the flow of air to slow the plane.

Madison opened her eyes.

The plane docked at the gate, the seat belt sign switched off, and everyone got up, gathering their things. Madison got her backpack from under the seat in front of her and exited the plane. Her eardrums felt funny, slightly muffled, like she'd been swimming and hadn't gotten all the water out of her ears.

She followed the rest of the passengers off the plane and down the airport corridors to the baggage claim, and there, standing by the carousel where the bags come out, she saw her mom and dad and Gina waiting for her. A wave of love and longing and gratitude for their familiar faces flooded through her, and Madison started running toward them. Before she was even halfway there, they saw her, and a split second later, Madison was surrounded and wrapped in a big family hug.

34
home again

"I still can't believe you didn't go to Disneyland," Gina said, shaking her head sorrowfully at Madison, like she thought her big sister had taken leave of her senses.

They were sitting at the kitchen table, and their dad was stirring some ground beef and onions in a frying pan on the stove. It smelled good. Madison was looking forward to her dad's spaghetti dinner. Just thinking about it made her mouth water.

"Ah well," Madison said, finding a piece of the jigsaw puzzle that was clearly the kitten's right ear and popping it into place.

"Are you sorry you didn't?"

"No," Madison said, rummaging through the remaining jigsaw pieces.

"I would be. If I went all the way to California and didn't get to go to Disneyland, I would cry for a very long time." Gina thought about that for a minute, then slid off her chair, padded around the kitchen table, climbed up into Madison's lap, and wrapped her arms around her big sister's neck. "Did you cry, Maddie?" she asked, tipping her head up and touching her nose to her sister's.

Madison smiled. Her little sister was a bit of a pest, but moments like this made it worth it. "No, Gina," she said, giving her sister a hug. "I didn't cry. It was my decision. Alyssa would have gone if I wanted, but we had more important things we needed to do."

"What," Gina asked, leaning back to look up at her big sister, "could possibly be more important than Disneyland?"

"Lots of things," Madison said.

Gina leaned in again, and Madison stroked her hair. Gina turned her face toward Madison's hand and sniffed. "Why do you smell like fish?" she asked.

Madison smirked, a memory of yesterday's triumph flashing before her.

"Oh drat!" Madison's father exclaimed. He was rummaging through the cupboard where they stored the canned goods. "What an idiot I am”—he straightened up and slapped his hand to his forehead—“I forgot to pick up some canned tomatoes.”

“No worries, Dad,” Madison said, plopping Gina off her lap and rising to her feet. “I’ll go to the store and pick it up.”

“You sure?” her dad asked. “You aren’t tired from the trip?”

“It will feel good to get back on my bike, to move a bit and get some fresh air. Do you need anything else?”

“No, just two large cans of crushed tomatoes.” He handed her a twenty-dollar bill from his wallet. “Thanks, chipmunk.”

Madison found the aisle with canned tomatoes, no problem. Shop & Save had discounted their in-store brand, and a large can of crushed tomatoes went for $1.29. Madison snagged two, made her way to the cashier, and got in line. There was a bit of an unpleasant smell. Madison was tempted to move, but already two more people were standing behind her, and all the other cashiers had long lines as well. She decided to stay put and breathe shallow.

“We had …” Madison heard from the next

line over, "the *most* fabulous time!" She knew that voice. "It was sunny the entire time. The weather was *amazing*. I got *such* a good tan." Madison went up on her toes and peeked over the top of the candy and magazine rack. It was Olivia. *Of course,* Madison thought as she plopped back down. *Who else would be bragging that loud? They must be back from their trip to Hollywood.* Olivia was with her mom, and Isabelle was there too, listening to Olivia with bated breath. "And the workshops were *divine*!" Madison giggled. She didn't even have to see Olivia's face to know what her exact expression was. "I met agents and real live professional actors, and there is a child manager who is *very* interested in me! Everything was perfection!"

"Well, not everything, dear," Madison heard Olivia's mother say. She sounded tired. Madison peeked over the rack again. Yup. She looked tired too. "There was that unfortunate incident yesterday on that Star Tours field trip."

Madison gasped.

Olivia's mom's head started to turn in her direction. Madison quickly dropped down so she was hidden by the rack, but her mind was spinning and her eyes were wide. *Oh my goodness! It couldn't be. No way!*

"Next."

The woman in line behind Madison nudged her. "Your turn, girlie."

"Oh, sorry." Madison put her cans of tomatoes on the conveyor belt and moved down the line, staring straight ahead, but keeping her ears alert.

"What unfortunate incident, Mrs. Vasbro?" Madison heard Isabelle ask.

"We were doing a tour of the homes of the stars," Mrs. Vasbro said, "when all of a sudden, outside of Jessica Ashton's gorgeous mansion, some sort of flying beast doused us with the most horrible-smelling stench. I don't know what it was, but my god, did it stink. It got in my hair, and I have shampooed three times since yesterday afternoon and still the smell lingers!"

Madison shoved her fist in her mouth to keep from laughing out loud. *Stuck-up Olivia and her fancy-dancy mom were sprayed with the smelly crawfish stink juice? Oh my god! Priceless. Alyssa is going to—*

"That will be two dollars and fifty-eight cents, please," the cashier said.

Madison got the money out from her pocket and handed it to the cashier. Madison's shoulders were shaking and her eyes watering with the effort of keeping the laughter in.

"Yes, actually," Madison heard Olivia say with a sniff, "that wasn't fun. I, personally, have never smelt anything so foul."

"Ooooh ..." Madison heard Isabelle say. "So that's what that smell is. I thought you were having a farting fit from the challenges of travel—different foods and all—so I didn't say anything."

"We don't smell *now*!" Madison heard Olivia say indignantly.

"Oh yes you do!" Isabelle replied earnestly. "Oww! Why did you whack me?"

"Are you all right, dear?" the woman behind Madison asked. "Do you have something stuck in your throat?"—she began rummaging in her large handbag—"I have a throat lozenge if you need it."

"No, thanks," Madison managed to squeak. "I'm fine."The cashier gave Madison her change, and Madison charged out of the store before she lost it all together.

Madison tied the plastic bag with the tomatoes to the handlebars of her bike. It took a bit longer than it should have because tears of laughter kept blurring her vision. Once the tomatoes were secure, she hopped on her bike and hightailed it out of there before Olivia and her mom came out of the store and demanded to know what was so funny.

After awhile, the laughter subsided, and Madison was left with a hole where Alyssa had been. She lifted up from the seat of her bike and pumped hard, trying to outrun the loneliness. She bent over the handlebars, feeling the burn in her legs, picking up speed, going faster and faster. It was a weird sensation to know that Alyssa and her mom weren't living in Rosedale anymore. The thought, that if she biked by their house, some other family would be living there now, was a depressing one.

Arf! Madison's head jerked up. *Grrrr … Arf!*

Oh no! There was Mrs. Bachrach's precious Pomeranian barrelling toward her with his gleaming white teeth bared and snapping.

Madison instinctually went into protective runaway mode and yanked hard on her handlebars, sending her bike into a U-turn. She would do what she always did when Rufus was on a rampage: go the long way around the block in order to get home. But as Madison finished the arc, an image of Alyssa's big Rottweiler, Nadine, flashed before her.

Arf … Rrrrrraughfff! Rufus, a snarling fluffball of fury, hurtled her way.

Enough! Madison thought. She wasn't running away anymore. She continued turning, a full 360 degrees, until she ended up with her bike facing Rufus head-on.

The dog hesitated for a second, momentarily

thrown, but then continued his dash forward—but not quite as fast as before. Which gave Madison courage.

She got off her bike, set the kickstand, and, standing tall, stared down the tiny ferocious slit-eyed fluffball.

"No," Madison said in a strong, decisive voice.

Rufus skidded to a stop. *Grrrr . . . arf . . .* Rufus was still trying to cling to his bad-guy stance, but Madison could tell he was confused.

Madison swelled her chest like she had seen Nadine do when she was about to go into fierce-guard-dog mode. Then she lifted her top lip, letting it vibrate slightly, showing all of her teeth as she released a low guttural warning growl.

Rufus sat, his gaze suddenly embarrassed, and then lowered himself to the ground.

Madison could hear the slap of Mrs. Bachrach's slippers as she huffed up the street toward them, but Madison didn't move and stayed in her ready-to-attack posture. "*Grrrrr . . .*" she growled again.

Rufus whimpered and rolled onto his back, showing his belly.

"What are you doing to my precious Rufus?" Mrs. Bachrach gasped.

"Teaching him some manners," Madison said, a wave of triumph surging through her. She was never, ever going to be terrorized by that little dog again.

She flung her leg over her bike, flipped the kickstand up, and pushed off. Mrs. Bachrach sputtered something, but Madison didn't stay to hear it. She had tomatoes to bring to her dad so they could have a tasty spaghetti dinner. She didn't have time to waste on Mrs. Bachrach and her badly behaved dog. She stood up out of her seat and pumped hard, the wind rushing past. She was Madison the victor—strong, powerful, and unafraid—and it felt good. *Just wait,* she thought, a huge smile on her face. *Just wait till Alyssa hears about this!*

acknowledgments

My heartfelt thanks to the many people who contributed to turning my manuscript into a book I am proud of. My first reader is always my husband, Don, my rock, my love. Next, a wheelbarrow of thanks goes to my brilliant literary agent, Laura Langlie, who is my second and third (and sometimes many more) reader. An author could not have a more dedicated, caring agent. The third powerhouse in this trifecta is my wonderful editor, Lynne Missen, whose sensitive editing suggestions made my manuscript a million times better.

I also thank the rest of the production team: Sandra Tooze, senior production editor; Chrystal Kocher, production coordinator; Helen Smith, editorial assistant; Eleanor Gasparik, whose credit is copyeditor, but who was so much more;

Liba Berry, proofreader; Catherine Dorton, cold reader; B.J. Weckerle, for the excellent formatting and interior design; Lisa Jager, for another exquisite cover design; Vikki VanSickle, publicist (and fellow middle-grade author of the Clarrisa books); and the entire Penguin Group sales force, who continue to work hard championing me and the other Penguin/Puffin authors.

My heartfelt gratitude to my readers for loving my novels almost as much as I do, and to booksellers for taking the time to read my books and those of other authors, and for knowing how to match them up with the right readers.

And last but not least, to librarians and teachers for introducing my books to your students: a BIG thank you, thank you, thank you!